THE SEALED TRUTH

A NOVEL

SRIJEET HALDER

ISBN: 978-93-5407-860-6

First paperback edition May 2020

facebook.com/thesealedtruth

ACKNOWLEDGEMENTS

It took immense patience and years of perseverance to complete this book. Therefore, I would like to thank the almighty God for giving me the strength and courage to take on this arduous journey.

I want to thank my wonderful parents for always supporting me. They left no stone unturned to give me the best education they could. Whatever I am today is because of them.

My beautiful wife, Rekha. She is my best friend, my beacon of hope, my biggest motivator who always pushes me to do the best in my life. She always believed in me, even during the bouts of self-doubt I had from time to time.

Rapidpress Publishing, for publishing this book and taking it to the hands of my readers.

Last but not least, my readers who chose this book. I hope you enjoy the story. Without his readers, an author is nothing but someone who knows how to type.

Optimus Parentibus

PROLOGUE

Delta Research Laboratory,
Chennai, India
Twenty Years Ago

"No…Nagasiva…You're hurting me."

"Can't control baby. You are so tempting."

"What if someone sees us?"

"Nobody is here. This place is locked for months."

It was eight in the evening. A few months back, at this time of the day, DRL would be filled with people. People in white coats conducting tests and writing reports, trying to solve the world's most challenging healthcare problems. DRL or Delta Research Laboratory was one of the leading research institutes in the country for medical research. In the supervision of one of its founders Dr. Gurudutt Gowda, DRL saw itself rising from dust to the pinnacle of the research & consultancy pyramid.

A few months back, an accident happened that forced DRL to shut down its operations indefinitely.

Nagasiva was the guard-on-duty at nights, whose shift ran from six in the evening to six in the morning. Recent desertedness in the lab has allowed him to bring his girlfriend from the nearby slum and have some adventurous nights.

Nagasiva was still a teenager who recently turned nineteen. He had studied till fifth grade, then ran away from school to play cards with his friends, day and night. When he turned fifteen, his father beat his ass with a big wooden stick. After that, Nagasiva never touched cards again.

After doing menial tasks here and there on daily wages, he found this job as a security guard through one of his elder brother's friend. He felt lucky to get this job. The money was okay, and all he had to do was be seated at the main gate till midnight when almost everybody left. Then he would make his bed near the compound wall and sleep like a log.

His girlfriend, Ponnammal, was fifteen and studied in the nearby government school. After being pursued by Nagasiva for weeks, she agreed to meet him alone. But that was a month back. It was their fourth meeting. She was hesitant at first, as she never explored her sexuality before. But Nagasiva was a perseverant lover. This was the first time when she was not here just to *meet*.

Nagasiva gave another bite at her neck. Ponnammal moaned as his teeth dug deeper. Suddenly, she heard something. "Wait," she requested.

Ignoring the request, Nagasiva started kissing all over her, travelling through the valleys and peaks of her body.

"I think somebody is here, Siva," she whispered.

He ignored her once again.

"Siva!! Stop it," she yelled and pushed him back.

Her sudden outburst pulled him out of the magical evolutionary spell he was in.

"I think somebody is there, Siva. Please go and check," she pleaded.

"Okay, fine. Stay behind me."

Then the sound came again, and this time they both heard it. It was the sound of some liquid dropping on the floor. They followed it to the main lab. The glass door of the lab was ajar, which was unusual because last time he came to check a couple of days back, it was closed. Nobody had entered the lab since then.

He entered the lab to find the source of the sound. The colour from his face immediately flushed when he snuck a peek inside the room. An old man, wearing black trousers and a blue-grey check shirt with cream coloured hand-woven sweater over it, lay on the floor face down. His shiny black scalp with two bushy tufts of grey hair on the sides of his head gave away his identity. He was Dr. Gowda. The boy trembled, his legs shaking as if they are no longer willing to support him. Unsure of what to do, he ran as fast as he could.

Half an hour later, two policemen entered the room, followed by the boy. One of them was sub-inspector Kapil. He couched on the floor to check the pulse of the man. There was none. The other man spotted an empty bottle of Botulinum Toxin, aka Botox, and a syringe lying on the table. Botox is produced by the bacteria Clostridium Botulinum which grows on stale food. It has a numbing effect on tissues, and when applied in a minuscule amount, it can relieve pain such as that originating from migraines. But injecting it intravenously in a significant amount can be fatal. It's one of the most lethal toxins known to humans.

It didn't require a detective's mind to understand what had happened there.

"Man trying to save the world killed himself," announced the newspapers the next day. Ironically, Prof Gowda was one of the proponents of using Botox for therapeutic purposes, who claimed it could be used to numb pain and improve skin appearance.

"Don't worry, Jaswant. I will rather die before I let anybody even touch this. But could you tell me now why are you in a hurry and where is your son," asked the man who had become the most promising star in the world of human psychology in the country. But the subject, who had been his friend for more than two decades, seemed beyond his comprehension right now.

"I trust you more than my life Adhusudhan. That is why I am giving you this responsibility. Just make sure that nobody comes to know about this until someone comes finding it."

"Who will come?"

"You will know."

"If that's what you want."

"I do," said Jaswant before turning back and running towards his car. He entered his car and drove away.

Adhusudhan stared at his friend's car speeding away from his doorstep.

CHAPTER ONE

Present Day, Melbourne Airport

Sitting at the plush sofa-chair of the business class lounge at Melbourne Airport, Sam remembers the day when his uncle trusted him the most responsible post of the company - Managing Director of Mehrotra Export and Import. "I am now retired, son, this company needs your enthusiasm. My old bones are no longer able to support its load," he had said. Sam, being himself an MBA from Melbourne Business School, never said that he could run the company better than his uncle. No one could run Mehrotra Export and Import better than Naresh Mehrotra himself. But when he succumbed to his pain due to a malignant brain tumour, he was sure that Sam would take the company to the pinnacle of the international trade business, where even he could not take it.

"Here you go," Zac handed the cup of hot latte to Samar, pulling him out of his reverie.

Despite being the son of the driver, Zac was never treated like a servant. He was regarded by Sam as well as his uncle, like Sam's own brother. When Naresh had brought Sam to his home in Melbourne, he was only five, and Zac was three. Zac and Sam grew up together, even went to the same school where Naresh was one of the trustees. Zac had always wanted to become a dentist, so he did.

Sam a.k.a. Samar Oza was an all-rounder – brilliant in academics, a champion in sports, and innovative when it came to business. Working as the CEO, Samar had taken his uncle's company to the next level. While his uncle had managed to link his company to many countries like South

Korea, Japan, and China, Samar, along with his uncle, took it as far as Moscow, Cuba, Bolivia, and Canada in just six years.

"Thanks, bud," smiled Sam.

A few minutes later, an announcement was made for the passengers of the flight from Melbourne to New Delhi. It was the cue for them to stand up and proceed for boarding.

"Mr. Samar Oza, your seat no. is 6B, and Dr. Zac Wilson, your seat no. is 5B. Please come with me," said the beautiful Australian air-hostess with a broad smile on her face. They placed their bags in the overhead bunker and took their respective seats.

"Gracias señora," said Zac to the hostess.

"You're welcome, Mr. Wilson," replied the *lady*. It was not the first time when Zac tried Spanish on a girl, and she understood and even answered. "Spanish is the language of love," he always said.

CHAPTER TWO

Office Of Beyond Horizon Consultants
Chennai, India
Present Day

Viren faced the building which had been his office for the last four years. Although an engineering graduate in Information Technology from Indraprastha University, New Delhi. After two years of futile attempts at joining any leading software firm. He landed up working in Beyond Horizon Consultants, who served people setting up their import-export business in India.

Being a senior executive, he was involved in acquainting new entrepreneurs with the prerequisites of setting up a new company. What nobody knew about him was that he wanted to become an entrepreneur himself.

He entered the building and looked down at his I-card in his hand, which stated, "Viren Shetty, Senior Executive," and exhibited a picture of him that seemed like it was taken when he was stoned. He handed over the card to the guard who returned it to him, not before scanning it into the computer. *The last attendance in Beyond Horizon,* he thought to himself.

With his entire mindset onto resigning the company on that day, he marched straight to the office of his boss, the Deputy General Manager of the company. He stopped at the desk of the secretary to the DGM and pulled out an envelope from his shoulder bag. He placed the envelope on her desk and asked her to give it to the boss. With that been said, he returned to his cubicle to start packing his belongings.

Only half an hour had passed when he was called by his boss.

"Sir, I am very grateful that you have accepted my letter so quickly," Shetty said as soon as he was permitted by his senior into his room.

"Mr. Shetty," Viren's boss started. He was a respectable man in his early forties. He led his team with respect and empathy. But out of everyone, he liked Viren most. All the clients that Viren handled were always delighted. His client praised him for being cooperative, polite, and meticulous in his job. The one thing Viren's boss didn't like in him was his reticence. He always found him a little sad as if he was missing something in his life. "I am very sorry I don't know what letter you are talking about," the DGM continued. "I have called you here to give *this* letter to you," he passed an envelope towards him.

"I don't understand, sir. What is it?" asked Shetty while scrutinizing the envelope from all fronts before opening it.

"Mr. Shetty, you have been promoted for the post of Associate Consultant, and this is your promotion letter. I had recommended you for this post to the GM a couple of months ago, but he couldn't take a look due to our financial year closing."

"That's kind of you, sir. I appreciate this from the core of my heart."

"That's nothing. It's all your hard work. But yeah, I want to tell you that new designation involves new responsibilities too. Next week you alone will be handling an Australian client who wants to expand their import-export business to India. You have to show them around and let them understand how things are done here. It is the first time that an already set up company is coming to us to expand its business further, so this can be an opportunity for us to take our company further up on the corporate ladder. That's why I wish you all the luck you need."

"Thank you, sir, I'll try my best to stand up to your expectations," replied Viren.

"And yeah, needless to say, this involves a hike of 20% of your salary too."

Viren smiled with a slight bow of the head and left the room. He noticed his resignation letter still lying on the desk outside the DGM's office. He took the letter and put it in his bag and left.

CHAPTER THREE

Sam and Zac had never visited India. Though Sam was born in India, he was only five when he lost his parents in a deplorable car accident. His uncle Naresh Mehrotra had just started an import-export firm after years of working as a freight operator at the Port of Melbourne. On receiving this ill-fated news, he came to India and flew back with his nephew. He loved Samar with all his heart and soul. He never even married because Samar was all he wanted as a family. The surname kept aside, Samar was his son in all respects.

Naresh considered Samar his lucky charm. Since the same month he brought Samar with him, his company got two new big contracts in Russia and South Korea. His company, which dealt with exotic handicrafts and artifacts, created a dozen new business alliances with big distribution companies as well as purchasing and manufacturing firms in the next year as compared to six last year.

Naresh Mehrotra grew up with his five years younger sister in Varanasi, which was considered the most sacred place in Hinduism as well as Jainism and Buddhism. Varanasi, according to Hindu scriptures, was founded by Lord Rudra. Buddha was believed to have founded Buddhism at this place. According to Garuda Puran, it was the holiest of the seven sacred places in India, which were also known as 'Sapt-Puri.'

Naresh was a Diploma holder in Agricultural Sciences from BHU – Benaras Hindu University. His father worked as a manager for landlords in Varanasi, then Benaras. When he was twenty-one, Naresh left home for Melbourne to make a living. With his friend, he illegally entered Australia in a cargo ship from Kolkata. In a nasty turn of events, he was betrayed and left to work at Port of Melbourne as a stevedore and later as a freight operator. After ten years of working as a freight operator, he finally went on to start his own import-export company. His hard-work, brilliance, and his ability to deal with people made his company's name go through the ceiling within a decade and a half.

Naresh's company dealt in all major markets around the globe, except India. When Samar had proposed to expand to India, Naresh told him that it's a too risky market. Samar didn't pursue the topic further. But when his uncle died, he decided to immerse Naresh's ashes into the Ganges in Varanasi, his birthplace. He took it also as an opportunity to explore the Indian market of handicrafts.

Varanasi, Uttar Pradesh
India
July 2013

When Sam disembarked from the train, he remembered all the stories his uncle had told him all these years about Varanasi. He was awe-struck when his uncle said to him that the city of Varanasi hosted more than twenty-three thousand small and big temples in an area that was smaller than Melbourne by a factor of six. He awed more when he was told that more than half of the temples from ancient times were destroyed by Qutub-din-Aibak and other Muslim rulers.

"Fuck off from me, you stupid beggars," Zac yelled at some beggars who surrounded him like ants attacking a dead cockroach devouring it into little chunks, which will serve them for the next winter. "Man! These guys are going to tear my clothes apart. Sam, do you care to help? You won't like to see me naked, I promise."

Sam fished out his wallet from his pocket and distributed some coins he got in change from the rail ticket booking office after purchasing two first-class tickets from New Delhi to Varanasi.

"What was wrong with those guys? They seemed perfectly normal. Two of them were even fitter than me. Why are they begging? And why did they not go after you but for me?" Zac asked, entirely intimidated by the scene.

"I think they liked your brown leather jacket," replied Sam mocking Zac's jacket, which he always called sexy among girls.

"What's wrong in this jacket? Girls are really into it. And it perfectly complements my dark brown hair," Zac defended.

"Well. After learning so much from my uncle, I know that Varanasi is considered a place of salvation. Hindus from all over the world come here to wash off their sins into the sacred river Ganga. They say that bathing into the river Ganga and making charity at this holy place makes you free from all your sins you committed in this as well as in the previous birth. I think that might be the basic business idea of these beggars. They charge you money for helping you get salvation," Sam explained to his still confused childhood friend.

Once in their hotel room, Samar took out an earthen pot covered with a red cotton cloth from the top. He watched it intently while tears welled up in his eyes. His uncle, all his wisdom, his kindness, and love now turned into ashes that he held in his hand inside a pot. *The ultimate destiny of all living beings,* " his uncle always reminded him whenever he missed his parents.

After getting fresh in their hotel room, they asked the receptionist for directions to Dashashwamedh Ghat. They were told to hire a manual cycle rickshaw that will take them to the place in no time.

After the long rickshaw ride that seemed like an eternity, they were left at a street which was full of people like a flock of sheep in suburban farmland. The moment Sam climbed down the rickshaw and the pot in his hand becomes visible to all, they were surrounded by men who wore a white cloth around their waist and carried a saffron shawl over their shoulder. They also wore a long white thread from one shoulder to the waist on the other side across the torso. They offered to help them perform the rituals regarding the immersion of the ashes called 'Antim-Sanskar.' They pulled the two guys from all sides. One of them almost snatched the earthen pot from Sam's hands.

They both were baffled and intimidated to their cores, and their faces did not hide anything. Thankfully, Sam was told by one of his Indian employees that his uncle was a Pandit in Varanasi, and if they ask for Ramashankar Sharma, they would be taken to him. After they get rid of all the annoying Pandits who offered them various schemes to help the dead reach the other world safely, they asked someone for Ramashankar Sharma. They were taken to his little cottage, where he seated in a silent posture with his legs folded and hands rested on the knees. He was nothing like the other Pandits, he was older and seemed calm and serene. Even with his eyes closed, he appeared to be watching all around.

The man, who brought them there, whispered in his ears, "Guruji, someone has come to meet you."

Guruji opened his eyes and watched the young boys and smiled. Like some retarded children, unsure of what else to do, they shone their teeth too.

"Guruji, I have come from Australia. My uncle Mr. Naresh Mehrotra passed away last week. I want to do his last rites."

"My child, death doesn't end the journey of a soul. In his journey, your companionship with him ended last week, but his journey has not ended."

Guruji's eerie voice left them speechless.

"I will go with you, and together we all will help your uncle leave this world and move to the other freely." Guruji stood up and continued, "thus completing a cycle of life and death."

Guruji, Sam, and Zac stood at the steps of the Dashashwamedh Ghat. The biggest ghat of Varanasi, Dashashwamedh Ghat, was famous for its proximity to the holy Vishwanath Temple and the 'Sandhya Aarti' or the evening prayer performed here every evening. People came here from all parts of India as well as abroad mainly to perform the last rites of the dead ones in the mother river Ganga.

"We have to go by boat to the middle of Ganga," announced Guruji and moved towards a boat waiting for passengers.

Samar and Zac followed without any questions.

A dark-complexioned man with a lanky figure wearing a half torn vest and a white dhoti rowed the boat. Zac watched the delicate arms of the boatman that moved back and forth. He wondered if a huge wave were to pass in the river right at the moment, what will break first – his arms or the oars. The boatman gave him a dirty look as if sensing his inner thoughts. Zac turned his gaze immediately to look at Guruji now. He sat at the opposite edge of the boat, chanting some muted hymns and counting his rosary beads.

When in the middle of the wide river, the boat came to a halt gradually, rocking up and down with the passing waves. Guruji stood up, followed by Sam and Zac. He took the pot from Sam and chanted some Mantras as he held it in his hands. He, then, touched it to his head and returned it to Sam. "Remove the cloth," he ordered.

Sam obeyed whatever said by Guruji.

"Drop the ashes into the water and repeat after me," Guruji ordered again and started chanting different Mantras. Taking his lead, Samar repeated the Mantras and slowly deposited all of the ashes into the water.

After that, Guruji gestured him to keep the pot aside and asked Sam, "What was your uncle's favourite food?"

Samar replied with Lady Finger.

"What your uncle wore mostly?" Guruji inquired.

"Shirt, trouser and coat," replied Samar.

"What were his favourite possessions?"

"His watch," replied Samar.

"Okay, now you have to send these things and a gold coin to your uncle along with your prayers. Otherwise, his soul won't be able to leave this world freely," Guruji paused for the young boys to understand and then started, "Speak after me. Hey, departed soul! I am providing you with all the things you need for your travel to the other land. I pray for your peaceful journey to paradise. May your soul rest in peace!"

Samar complied with him and repeated his words.

"Now you have to give me fifty thousand rupees," Guruji said flatly.

"What!!!?" Samar and Zac exclaimed in unison.

"It is for the things you just sent to your uncle?"

"But this is nonsense. How will you actually send these things to him?" demanded Sam.

"This is all written in the Shastras. You cannot question it, else you will be damned, and your uncle will be burned in hell," Guruji spoke with a rage.

Zac watched the boatman, his expression spoke clearly that if they were not to pay the money, they would be left in the middle of the river.

"But I cannot pay you such amount, this is just insane," Samar said sheepishly.

"Now you have sent those things to your uncle, and I have also helped you. If you don't pay for it, you will be haunted by the evil."

Sam realized they were cornered, and they were not in a position to do anything other than complying with him.

"But I have only forty thousand in Indian currency with me right now," Sam gave his last attempt on a bargain.

"Well……..Naresh was my good friend. I can pay for the rest of it. You can pay me forty thousand," Guruji said with a condescending voice as if he was doing the biggest charity in the world.

Sam reluctantly took out the money from his wallet and handed it over to him.

"May God bless you, my son," Guruji said, putting his hand on Sam's head. "Your uncle feels very proud of you now. You will always be blessed by him,"

Zac laughed till his stomach hurt, on their way towards the Varanasi airport in their hired cab. He eyed Samar briefly and started laughing again. The cab driver looked into the mirror and wondered if the 'firangi' had gone crazy.

"Come on, man, stop now," Samar elbowed on his arms. Zac was extremely exhilarated by the cunning act of robbery conducted on them by the Guruji. Though Samar did not laugh it loud, he still was having a hard time to put the grin off his face.

"I have to agree, Sam, I am falling in love with India," Zac put it out in his husky Australian accent.

"Oh come on, don't tell me you were never mugged in Melbourne."

"Well yeah, I was once, but that was just silly. Two guys pointed a machete at me, and I was forced to give my money to them. But this was ingenuity. If you are a little too pietistic, you will be robbed of your clothes, and you will never know it," Zac smirked, and Sam knew he was right. Sam, though not an atheist, never believed in these orthodox traditions or in the theories like reincarnation, or sinners burning in hell. He called them groundless and believed that they were designed by ancient intellectual people to keep the general public on the right path.

"My uncle had always told me that India was once one of the most intelligent and richest countries in the world. But two hundred years of slavery and poor politics faced by the country have corrupted the moral consciences of its people," Samar watched Zac listening to him carefully.

"Have you heard about Vedic Mathematics?" demanded Sam.

"Hmm…..I think no," Zac replied, genuinely trying to remember if he really had.

"Vedic Maths is now being researched by various researchers. Vedic maths is the maths of Vedas. There are four Vedas in India which were written thousands of years ago. It is said that Vedic Maths in its full power could solve Mathematical problems involving addition, subtraction, multiplication, differentiation, simultaneous equations, complex numbers, and more within a few seconds."

"Fascinating!"

"Do you know one of the verses that Guru was chanting was Gayatri Mantra. My uncle had taught me about it. In Vedic Maths, big numbers were represented by the Sanskrit alphabets, as we now use English alphabets in hexadecimal systems in computer programming. And the Gayatri Mantra when decoded adds up to 108," Sam smiled.

"What's so special in the number 108?" Zac asked with real curiosity.

"108 is a number which appears in many scriptures, sages use rosary of 108 beads for chanting god's name, 108 lamps are lighted during special prayers."

"But what's so important in that number?"

"It's a cosmological number. The distance from the earth to the sun is 108 times the diameter of the sun. And the distance from the earth to the moon is also 108 times the diameter of the moon. Did you know that Julius Robert Oppenheimer, the father of the Atomic Bomb, was heard quoting 'The Bhagavad Gita' on first testing of the Atom Bomb?"

"Really?"

"He was a student of Sanskrit and had studied 'The Bhagavad Gita,' 'The Mahabharata' and other Indian scriptures, and had cited many Indian archaeological sites. When asked from him if the atomic test at Alamagordo was the first nuclear test. He replied, 'Yes, in modern times.' Even a lot of evidence has been found in ancient scriptures as well as from archaeological investigations, suggesting there was nuclear warfare in ancient India."

Zac nodded in admiration.

"It is pretty clear that the ancient Indians were smartass. But as the country got invaded by many foreigners over the history such as Alexander, Persians, Mughals, et al., it lost its vast pool of knowledge and was thrown into darkness. But to quote my uncle 'once fallen rise again,' he believed that this country will rise once again and rule the whole world. But we won't be lucky enough to see that day. Our grandchildren might be."

Zac listened intently to each word Sam had to say.

Sam smiled, amused. "I wonder how you haven't asked me yet about where we are headed," he said.

"I thought we are moving back to Melbourne, aren't we?" Zac replied and frowned in confusion.

"No, pal, not so soon. We are heading down to Chennai," Sam revealed.

"Chennai!! Where's that, and why so?" Zac demanded.

"It's the capital of Tamil Nadu state of India. All the way down to the southernmost part of the country. We have to change flight from New Delhi with a four-hour waiting there, will take about eight hours in total," explained Sam before turning to the driver, "How long to the airport, brother!"

"Less than a kilometer, sir," returned the driver.

"But why are we going to Chennai?" Zac begged again.

"My uncle always used to tell me various things about India and its rich cultural heritage. I had seen some really admirable pieces of exotic handicrafts exported from India. But whenever I asked my uncle to join some links here, he refused. He admitted that Indian handicrafts were second to none, yet he didn't want me to do business here. I believe he had some really harsh memories with this country. But he never gave me a good reason to refrain from setting up a business here. But my advisors have warned that doing business here could be really tricky as the way of conduct here is little tweaked. So we need to be careful."

"That's great, Sam, but the question remains unchanged. Why Chennai?" Zac demanded.

"It's because Chennai is the nearest port from Australia, and Tamil Nadu is very rich in handicrafts. I have contacted a consultancy firm that deals with import-export companies like us to help set out the strategies of work in India, especially Chennai. We are meeting them tomorrow. We will collect some data and move back to Melbourne in three days, where I will discuss the feasibility and risks of this venture with our market analysts. If we manage to extract a practicable amount of profit from here, I, along with my lawyer, will fly back to Chennai to sign a deal in two or three months," Sam explained to his friend.

Moments later, their car stopped at the entrance of Lal Bahadur Shastri Airport or the Varanasi Airport. They disembarked from the vehicle and paid the driver with a generous tip and disappeared behind the airport entranceway.

CHAPTER FOUR

Chennai, India

Piyu woke up with her alarm. She pulled her mobile out from under her pillow and dismissed the alarm to stop the forceful vibrations of her week-old smartphone. She read the '9:00 AM - Call Mom' reminder before putting the phone back to its place. She rubbed her face and forced herself up. She tied her hair into a bun and turned to look at the other side of the bed, where Vishal was still sleeping face against her.

She slipped out of the cover and searched for her clothes. Once she found her bra and her briefs, she walked straight into the bathroom and called her mom.

"Hi, Mom!" replied Piyu looking into the mirror and rubbing her eyes.

"Hi, baby! Where were you yesterday? You said you will call me," her mom replied from Melbourne.

"Sorry, mom, was a little busy yesterday. Some of the last paperwork was to be done in college. That's why I set a reminder to call you this morning," Piyu hated lying to her mom. In truth, she was with Vishal. She wished to call her mom at around 1 in the night when it would be early morning in Melbourne. But that time, Vishal could not get his hands off her. It was after a month and many insisting calls from Vishal when she visited him at his home again. After eleven months of relationship with him, she found out that they were at different places in the relationship.

Piyu a.k.a. Preyakshana Mishra was an ambitious girl. Her parents, Australian NRIs, sent her to do an MBA from the

Indian Institute of Management – Tiruchirappalli, where her father had also studied from. She had always been an independent girl, and despite her father being in a very influential position inside the corporate world, she wanted to climb the business ladder on her own.

Vishal ran his ancestral restaurant on the East Coast Road in Chennai and made a splendid fortune out of it. He had always been the dominating one in their relationship. He had been the do-this-don't-do-that kind of a boyfriend the whole time they were together, and now he had been asking Piyu for a real commitment for the last two months.

"Okay, beta! I was just worried about you? When are you heading back?" her mom asked eagerly.

"Very soon, Mamma, very soon. But now I have to go, have some work to do," replied Piyu.

"Okay, beta! Take care of yourself. Call me again in a day. Bb-bye."

"Bye, Mamma. Love ya."

"Love you too, beta."

Piyu hung up.

When Piyu returned into the room, she found Vishal sitting on the bed.

"Good Morning," wished Piyu.

"Good Morning, cherry" Vishal smiled at her.

She kissed him on his cheeks and sat beside him.

"What will you have for breakfast?" he asked.

"Juice and an omelet, if it's not big a deal for you," she said.

"Not at all, baby," he picked up his boxers and slipped into it. "I'll come in a minute," and left the bedroom.

Ten minutes later, he returned with the breakfast tray and placed it on the bed.

She tasted the omelet and took a sip from the glass of juice.

"You know what, baby?" he started after taking a sip from his glass. "Thanks for the last night. I was apprehensive about where this relationship is going. Now I have no doubts about this anymore," said Vishal enthusiastically.

"Really? How?" Piyu frowned.

"Because you are finally committed to me," he smiled.

"What!! When did I say so?" she asked, confused.

"Last night. While making love. When I asked you if you will marry me and you said yes," he uttered, worried now.

"But how could I say that? I haven't even thought about it yet," she said, embarrassed.

"But you want to marry me someday, don't you?"

"*Vishal!* For the last time, I haven't really thought about it yet," she cried, getting irritated now.

"But why *can't* you? It has been almost a year now, I find you perfect for me, and I think I too am perfect for you. I am not asking you to marry me today but commit to me, at least. And what's the problem? You completed your MBA a month ago. I have offered you the post of the manager in my restaurant. What's left then?" he said exasperated.

"Let me make it very clear to you, Vishal! It's my call to decide who is perfect for me. And I have told you earlier that I have my whole career in front of me. I cannot get into a serious relationship right now, nor in the foreseeable future. So stop pestering me for this nonsense," she said, utterly annoyed.

"So now you think our relationship is nonsense. The whole year we spent together was nonsense. If you didn't want to have a serious relationship with me, then what did you want? Or just sleeping in my bed is all you wanted?"

words fell through his mouth without filtering through his brain. But *Errare Humanum Est-To err is human*

"What the fuck!! What a jerk you are? And who the hell of a guy asks a girl to marry him when having sex?" she yelled at him.

"And who the hell of a girl keeps fucking a guy but refuses to marry him. Oh yeah! I know who, they are called sluts," he regretted immediately saying that, but the damage had already been done.

There was a long pause.

She finally broke the silence and said, "I am leaving for Melbourne next month,"

He said nothing.

"I don't think it's working anymore," Piyu wondered if she had made the right decision.

"Does it mean?" he stopped to let her utter the final words.

"It's over now, I am sorry," she stood up, collected her clothes and went into the bathroom. Fifteen minutes later, she came out fully dressed up in a blue tank top and a white trouser. Tears rolled on her fair cheeks.

She looked around the bedroom, but Vishal was nowhere to be seen. She left the room and found him standing at the main door. She opened the door for herself when he spoke *his* final words, "You know what? I know that the whole career thing is bullshit. If you wanted to sleep around, you should have told me straight, bitch!"

She didn't respond and left his house *forever*.

CHAPTER FIVE

The Assistant General Manager put the receiver down. "He will be here in no time," he smiled at the two gentlemen sitting in grey suits across the rectangular glass-top table. "Would you like to have some tea or coffee?" he requested his guests.

"Maybe coffee," replied the man on the right.

"Very well," the AGM said. He pressed a button on the telephone and spoke, "Send in three coffees."

In no time, a pantry boy entered the room, carrying a tray with three cups. He placed one cup before each of the suited men and one before the AGM and left as silently as he came.

"Well, Mr. Oza, I need to tell you, you have visited us on an exceptional day. We have turned 25 today, and our company is making a small celebration at the company's beach house. We would like to invite you to celebrate our success," the AGM spoke enthusiastically.

"That's so kind of you, Mr. Kher. Many congratulations on your company's 25th anniversary and we will be delighted to be a part of your celebrations," replied Samar Oza.

There was a knock on the door, "May I come in, sir?"

"Oh yeah, Mr. Shetty, please join us," the AGM welcomed the newly designated senior executive of the company.

Sam and Zac turned to watch the young man entering the room. Sam noticed that the young man wore the same neck-tie as him. He smiled at the coincidence.

The AGM, noticing the same, uttered exultantly, "It seems like our senior executive shares the same taste in fashion with you, Mr. Oza."

Everyone chuckled.

"Mr. Oza, this is our senior executive Mr. Viren Shetty. He will be handling your case. He will show you the presentations and provide you all the data as well as introduce you to the different rules and regulations of our country regarding international trade." He added, "I must tell you he is one of the most talented and hard-working employees of our company. And you will really enjoy his company."

"And Mr. Shetty, this is Mr. Samar Oza, M.D. of Mehrotra Exports & Imports and his friend Mr. Zac Wilson. They want some analytics solutions for expanding their business to India. I had mailed you the details a week ago. Please make sure Mr. Oza meets all his requirements. And also do check that a formal invitation for today's party reaches their hotel suite."

"Yes, definitely, sir," replied Viren with a little bow.

"Thank you, Mr. Kher. It was a pleasure meeting you," Samar stood up and extended his hand towards the AGM.

"Pleasure was all mine, Mr. Oza. Thank you, Mr. Wilson," he shook their hands and bade them goodbyes.

Viren escorted them to the company's conference room on the same floor of the building, and uttered, "Sir, I have been analyzing your data for the last seven days. Apparently, you are an Export Management Company-cum-Distributors dealing in Exotic Handicrafts."

"That's right," replied Sam.

"It means you associate with manufacturers, identify potential buyers for them, and facilitate shipping and warehousing of their products. It's that, right?"

Sam nodded in consent.

"Very well, sir. It appears that, though your company has originated from Australia, yet it's no longer its base country. You deal with manufacturers and buyers in almost all the continents and move their goods to-and-fro without even passing through Australia," asked Viren, opening a presentation on his laptop, which was then reflected on the large screen via a projector.

"That's right. We had noticed in very early stages of our business that there's the demand for a certain type of exotic handicrafts in certain countries. While some like pottery, they didn't like stonework. Similarly, while sellers of some country specialized in woodwork, yet there was a lack of suppliers who specialized in metal-engraved artifacts."

Viren gave a contemplative nod. Zac, bored to his core, looked through him.

"Sir, I have researched the Indian market thoroughly for the potential sellers as well as the buyers for the products your company deals with. I have shortlisted quite a few companies," he scrolled down to the slide of the presentation, which showed names of several companies dealing in exotic handicrafts. It also showed their corresponding turnover and domain in the Indian market.

He continued, "Our research team has already forwarded questionnaires to the shortlisted companies, demanding the scale of their business, the range of the area covered by their distributors and market shares. We have also requested them to fill a column stating whether they have the capacity as well as interest to exhibit their products in the global market."

Sam smiled in admiration. He knew Viren had trimmed a substantial portion of the work, thus reducing almost a month of work in their part. Unlike other countries, Sam had considered for the first time to seek advice from a consultancy to set up a branch of their business in India. It would appear as only an itsy-bitsy dot in their huge balance-sheet. However, it now seemed like it would save a lot of work on their part, thus making it an overall profitable venture.

"I have also studied the prevailing prices in the market and the tax structure regarding the off-shore trading of the kind of products you deal in."

Viren continued for almost an hour, presenting different graphs, tables, and charts, giving statistical insight into the possible out turns of the proposed venture. Meanwhile, he watched Zac dozing off several times during the presentation. He rested his head over his palm and woke up alarmed whenever his head slid over his palm and fell out of it. Sam followed Viren's gaze and noticed him too. He gave out a mirthful smile to Viren, who smiled back as much as he could without risking an insult to his client's friend.

"Come on, man. How much sleep do you need in a day?" Sam nudged his friend, who covered his face inside the blanket. He turned again to face the large mirror in their suite, blowing his hair dry. He had just finished his bath, and a blue towel draped around his waist. His well carved muscular body glistened in the yellow light glowing above the full-length mirror. The scent of his exotic body-wash percolated through the bathroom and diffused into the bedroom air.

Sam had spent the entire day discussing various aspects of his new venture. He had called his managers in Melbourne, relating them all the primary details of his meeting in the office of Beyond Horizon Consultants. After spending better hours of the day, he finally retired to their hotel with Zac. Zac, tired to the core, fell asleep as soon as he settled himself in one of the plush ultra-comfortable bed of the suite. He lay on his belly with his face buried in the feather-soft mattress. It gave him a feeling as he was floating on air, and there was no ground below, but a blow of wind forceful enough to hold him there as well as gentle enough to let him sleep. He covered his face with the white satin blanket. Zac, though a fully mature adult, slept like a toddler.

"I thought you had had your sleep during the meeting?" Sam asked playfully.

"Please don't even speak about that," Zac replied groggily with his face still covered by the blanket. "When you said 'We will have fun in India,' I had thought here will be touring, boozing, and girls. You didn't tell me that it would be boring lectures once again, like in college."

"Come on, man. My uncle has just passed away. How can we…"

"Okay, I'm sorry, I was just kidding. But I'm not going into your boring meeting tomorrow. I have a huge jet lag to cope up with. I will better sleep my whole day off tomorrow."

"I thought you had handled your jet lag yesterday in Varanasi," Sam replied, dressing his hair with the comb.

"I had almost, and then you made me travel once again, here to Chennai."

"How on earth does a flight within the same time zone cause you a jet lag? Even Melbourne has only five and a half-hour time difference from India. You are being a sissy,"

"Oh yeah," Zac snapped, pulling the blanket down his face. "Then you have become an uncle who keeps complaining all the time. Hah!" he chuckled.

Sam opened his mouth to say something when the doorbell buzzed. He put his gown on and pulled out the towel from beneath and went on to open the door.

"Oh, hi, Viren! What brings you here? I thought your office hours ended at five," Sam noticed Viren was wearing a shiny black suit with a glazy neck-tie over a plain white shirt which appeared to be brand new. He then suddenly remembered the anniversary party of Beyond Horizon, which they were invited in by the manager earlier that day.

"Sir, as you have already been intimated about the twenty-fifth anniversary of our company today. I am here to invite you for the party," he handed him a small bouquet of orange roses. To the bouquet, hung a rather big cream-colored folder made of handmade paper. "A car is waiting downstairs with a chauffeur. Here is the valet ticket. You should show it to the valet attendant, the car will be brought to you and take you to the party venue near Uthandi Beach. It's only fifteen minutes' drive from here."

"Thank you, Mr. Viren. Your company knows very well how to handle clients," Sam winked at the executive.

"We are only doing our duty, sir. In India, a very famous proverb goes like '*Atithi Devo Bhava*' which means the Guest is God."

Sam silently admired the Indian courtesy.

"I, on behalf of our company, request you to honour our party with your presence," Viren uttered with a slight bow of the head.

"Well. We will, on one condition," Sam replied suddenly with a grim voice.

"And that would be, sir?"

"You have to stop calling me Sir, at least out of the office. I am almost your age. You calling me Sir makes me look like an uncle," he turned to look towards his bedroom to check if Zac was listening. He snored like a tractor. "It's a new place for us, and we would like to make a friend rather than a business associate."

"Very well, sir…I mean, Mr. Oza," Viren replied sheepishly.

"Just call me Sam or Samar if you will," Sam smiled and offered a hand.

"Yes, Samar. Hope to see you at the party," he smiled back and shook his hand and turned to leave.

Sam closed the door and opened the folder. He pulled out a fancy invitation card. To it, a small box of Pierre Cardin was tied with a ribbon. "You are invited to attend the 25th anniversary of Beyond Horizon Consultants" card announced in a huge fancy font, along with the venue and the timing of the party.

After an hour, Sam stood at the main entrance of their hotel. He had finally managed to coax Zac to accompany him to the party. He had handed the valet ticket to the attendant and waited for their vehicle to arrive.

They turned towards the driveway when the attendant announced, "Mr. Oza, your car has arrived."

Zac looked at the car and whispered in amazement, "This Company has a taste in cars." His gaze fixed in awe at the shining black BMW 740Li that stood in front of them.

CHAPTER SIX

Sam and Zac entered the beach house. The main entrance was on the opposite side of the beach. They entered through the main door where they were welcomed by the company staff. They walked a few steps through a narrow corridor that turned right to end into the main hall.

The hall was filled with people, mostly in black suits. Sam turned his gaze to watch everyone standing, talking, and holding drinks. Although Sam had attended many corporate parties like this with his uncle, Zac was not yet accustomed to them. Zac also turned his head slowly to look at everyone, he checked the girls who were the daughters of various businessmen. Some stood with their mothers, while some made groups among themselves.

"Welcome! Welcome, Mr. Oza! I have been waiting for you till yet," Mr. Kher, the AGM of the company, approached them from their right. "Would you like some snacks?" he offered as he shook hands with the two young men.

"No, thank you. We are not hungry just as yet," replied Sam.

"Anyways, please enjoy the party. There is a bar at the sea-side. The way there is at the end of this hall. We hope you like our hospitality. If you need anything, our staffs are at your service."

"Sure, Mr. Kher," Sam replied with a formal smile. The AGM left to entertain the other guests.

"Wanna get some drinks?" asked Zac, already making his way towards the end of the hall.

"Yeah, sure. This side of the party seems to be dull. Perhaps, the other side hosts some fun there," Sam said as he followed his friend to the sea-side.

Standing at the beach, they noticed the party be all too different from that inside. In stark contrast to inside, there was some soft music, the people seemed to be more energetic, and more importantly, they were far younger. Leaving their business tycoon fathers inside, the young ones were partying outside. Girls were wearing short dresses, guys holding glasses of wine, cocktail, and other poisons.

Sam spotted Viren, who was waving towards them. He smiled at him and waved back. Soon, Viren approached them and spoke, "Welcome, sir, how do you like the party?"

Sam arched his left eyebrow.

"Oh, I mean Sam."

Sam smiled and said, "We have just joined the party. We are yet to discover all the surprises."

"Well, Sam, to be frank, I must tell you there isn't any. These corporate parties are designed to be simplistic and plain without any surprises."

"I thought it's only the case in Australia, I thought Indians are far more fun-loving," Sam replied jocosely.

"Then, you have to stay a few more days and let me show you the fun side of India."

"Well, it's done then. After tomorrow's meeting, you are showing us the real India. We can tell your boss that we are leaving for some market research. Our flight is on Thursday, and today's just Monday. So you get plenty of time to prove to me that I was not wrong earlier."

"It's a deal, sir, I mean Sam," said Viren.

"Never mind! I think you are going to make me bored calling me sir all the time," said Sam gravely.

"No. It won't happen again. I promise," Viren winked and continued, "Let me introduce you to my friend." He turned to find her friend at some distance, standing in front of the bar, "There she is."

They followed Viren to the bar. A girl in her early twenties leaned against a tall, round glass table, lighted with a blue hue from below. Her curly brown hair and fair complexion with pouty pink lips made her resemble the teen pop star, Miley Cyrus. She wore an elegant orange tube dress. She took the final sip of martini from the conical glass in her hand. She noticed the three men approaching her and straightened up. Her face lighted up in amazement when she recognized *two* of them.

"No way!! I was just thinking about you a few days back. And now you stand here right before me, that too at a place where it was most unexpected. What a small world," Piyu uttered in complete amazement.

"You guys already know each other?" asked Viren, surprised. Samar smiled at the second coincidence of the day.

"Of course, we know each other. We have known each other ever since we were born. Or at least since *I* was born, for Sam was born five years before me," Piyu spoke enthusiastically.

Viren smiled and frowned alternately in wonder.

"Well, to end the suspense, let me add some information here," Sam raised his hand as he said, "Piyu is the daughter of Mr. Surajmal Mishra owner of Peacock Arts & Crafts (PAC) Ltd. It has become one of the leading distributors of imported handicrafts in Melbourne, Adelaide, and other Australian cities. Mr. Surajmal and my uncle Naresh Mehrotra had been dealing together since the very first year of Mehrotra Exports & Imports. Piyu and I had met several times at parties or informal meetings at our place or hers."

"And to add some more, Sam had also been my tutor when I was preparing for MBA. It was his invaluable help, by which I was able to get admission in IIM."

"But you never told me that your name is Piyu also. I thought it's just Preyakshana," Viren intervened.

"Actually, it was little professional here, so I thought it would be good to keep my pet name at home," Piyu pouted her lower lip.

"Well then, here's just one person left for the introduction, Mr. Wilson," said Viren pointing towards Zac.

"Yeah, Piyu, this is Zac, my friend, my brother. He lives with me now in Melbourne at my place."

To the oblivion of Sam and Piyu, Zac had seen Piyu on several occasions at Sam's house. At some point in their childhood, he had even developed a crush on her. This was not just a silly teenage infatuation, but something profound. Unfortunately for him, he was never introduced to her. Eventually, he somehow managed to suppress his feelings. He still remembers the day when she passed by him wearing a graceful white Cinderella dress. It was more than fifteen years back during a party at Sam's house.

"Hi! Pleasure meeting you," Piyu extended her hand.

He shook her hand. It was the first time she touched him. The warm, mesmerizing touch of her skin left Zac spellbound. The amorous feeling for her, which he had buried somewhere deep in his heart, was dug out again by her mere touch. Desperate to say something more, he opened his mouth, but to his bad luck, only a deep, loud sigh left his lips. But fatefully, no one seemed to notice that he was spared the embarrassment.

"Though I knew you are living in Chennai, yet it surprises me to meet you on our very first day in the city. Small world indeed!" Sam turned towards Viren, "How *you* two know each other?"

"Actually, I met him six months back at the office of BHC," Piyu butted in, Sam turned towards him. "I was appointed as an intern under his mentorship. Since then, we have been good friends. Today, when he invited me to this party, I had nothing better to do in my mind, so I agreed readily."

Viren smiled at her. She smiled back. What they failed to notice was that Zac was staring at her constantly without even blinking once. He wanted to satiate his sense of sight with her view as much as he could. He didn't know when he would be able to lay his eyes on her face next.

"I have requested Viren to be our guide for two days and show us around the city. Thankfully, he has agreed. Would you too like to join us?"

"Fuck yeah, why not? I have been here for more than two years now but not yet taken a tour of the city."

Sam and Viren chuckled. "You will never change," said Sam.

She winked.

Zac still stared at her, intently watching her curled eyelashes lined with a sleek black eyeliner. Her subtle orange eye-shadow complimented her orange dress. He noticed her bright grey eyes, he wondered if they were natural or she wore eye-lenses, as he never got to watch her so closely before then. He watched her long brown curly hair being flown with the cool breeze of the sea. She looked mesmerizing. *Wake up, Zac, wake up* he mutely shouted to himself. His brain continually demanding the control of his body, but his heart had hi-jacked it, leaving him paralyzed. After a long war between his heart and mind, his mind finally got the control back.

He noticed her looking at him now. *Come on, Zac, speak up, speak up.* He finally managed to open his mouth and say, "Are you really coming with us tomorrow?"

The meeting on the next day was painfully similar to that on the other day. There was but an exception of Zac sitting straight and constantly staring in the direction of the projector screen, unlike the previous day when he slumped on his chair. Sam was amused to see Zac taking an interest in the meeting. Only if he had the slightest hint that Zac didn't watch the change of slides on the screen, but the sluggish motion of the hand of the wall clock above the screen. It showed a quarter past noon.

After what appeared to be an eternity to Zac, he watched the projector screen go blank at around quarter to three. He knew it meant the end of the meeting. A smile crossed his lips as he watched Viren put his cell phone down and announce, "Piyu is on her way, she'll be here in no time. Then we can leave for a tour of the city."

CHAPTER SEVEN

The foursome filled Viren's small company-issued Hyundai Santro. It had zero luxuries, but Zac didn't mind travelling even on a donkey's back as long as Piyu was there. Sam, just as his uncle, never favoured luxuries over friends. Sam volunteered to sit beside Viren, who drove the car. This allowed Zac to sit with Piyu on the rear seat.

"I have already started loving India," stated Zac plainly.

Sam and Piyu chuckled as Viren cranked up the engine to start.

They roamed around for the rest of the day, visiting various tourist spots. They visited the famed temple of Mahabalipuram fifty kilometre outside Chennai city.

On their return, the place that amused Zac immensely was the Crocodile bank that housed hundreds of crocodiles, among other reptiles such as snakes and turtles. Zac loved reptiles. His bedroom walls were lined with pictures of him holding a variety of lizards. When he was eight, he had cried for weeks because his young Gecko died from Cryptosporidium parasitic infection. On his insistence, his father performed all the cemeterial rituals for his deceased friend.

Piyu, on the other hand, was intensely herpetophobic. She couldn't bear the sight of a lizard or anything that has a tail and crawls, leave alone a giant crocodile or alligator. She didn't even put a foot out of the car when she saw the entrance board of 'Madras Crocodile Bank Trust.' Zac and Piyu were polar extremes when it came to affection towards reptiles. Zac was really disheartened by this knowledge.

They travelled around the city till late in the evening. They left the beaches for the next day since Piyu wanted to spend a whole day at the beach as she did every month at St. Kilda Beach in Melbourne when she was young. Her father would open a barbecue while she played, bicycled, and danced with her mother and her two cousins Rani and Nisha. Her cousins accompanied her since their separated parents never took time out of their busy schedules for the kids. She loved her cousins.

Piyu made Viren stop at the Express Avenue Mall. She shopped as someone possessed, buying anything and everything that caught her eyes.

"So, what's the plan now? We still got four hours for the day to end. Anything left to see in here?" asked Zac leaning against the right-side rear door of the car. He didn't want the day to end ever. They waited in their car in the parking of the mall for their next destination to be planned up. "Let's go pubbing, shall we? Done with the day, we should check out the night of the city too. What say?" offered Zac, still not having his share of looking at Piyu for the day.

"I say it's cool," Piyu raised her hand, Zac gave her a High-Five.

"Actually guys, Viren and I have a lot of work to do tomorrow. We got a long list of suppliers to contact and discuss our plans with. We will have to start early in the morning. So no booze tonight," Samar said.

Piyu pouted.

"I was hoping I would take a look at my parents' old house in this city," Sam added.

"Your parents lived in Chennai?" Viren asked, surprised.

"I was born and brought up until the age of five in Chennai. After my parents passed away, my uncle took my custody, thus, getting me Australian citizenship. Since I am a PIO, I can stay here as long as I want with no visa."

"And this old house of your parents, where is it?"

"As told by my dear uncle, it's in Anna Nagar East, Chennai. I have the full address in my phone."

"Oh, wow! What a coincidence, I reside in the same neighbourhood. I can show you that place, and later I want all of you to have dinner with my family," Viren hoped he didn't offend his high-class businessmen friends by inviting them to his middle-class house. As far he came to know his new mates, none of them had even a trace of an ego. Not for even once, they made him realize that he was just a regular employee of a local Indian company, and they were some Australian resident business tycoons or daughter of a high-profile businessman.

"Let's do that way then," announced Sam loudly.

"Okay. Then sit tight. It's a half an hour drive from here. Take in the cool breeze of Chennai till then." Viren cranked up the engine and pulled the car carefully through the narrow exit of the underground parking lot.

Later in the night, after checking his parents' house, Sam, along with his friend, was welcomed in Viren's home by his mother, father and his elder brother Pankaj. After having a stomach full of tasty desi dinner prepared by Viren's mother, the quartet moved to the terrace accompanied by Pankaj.

Sam noticed that the housing society titled as the DBS Apartments located in the 1st Ave Road was a rather posh apartment for a newly joined employee of a small private firm. He and his four-years elder brother, who mentioned to be an insurance agent working on a commission basis with the most prominent public sector insurance company of the country, could not afford such a luxurious apartment. It didn't require a long time experience in the Indian real estate business to notice such obviousness.

"Umm…Viren! Did you live here since childhood?" Sam demanded.

"No, actually, we shifted here four years back. Pankaj has been working here for seven years now. It's not until I took the job in BHC, my parents and I shifted here permanently."

"I want to know what would be the price of that old house we saw today. It's no point keeping that house locked forever. Maybe someday I would like to sell it to someone who can put it to better use."

"I can't tell you for sure. But my brother can tell you more accurately. What say, *bhaiya*?" Viren passed the question to his *elder brother*.

"Which house are you talking about? Is it here in Anna Nagar?" Pankaj waited for more details.

"It's a medium size villa at the New Avadi Road. Right opposite to the Trinity Church. 2500 square feet would be my best guess. It was kept locked for twenty years."

"Did you say Trinity church," Pankaj frowned. "Is it the Shankar Villa, the one in the yellow and white colour, having two baby angels mounted on each flank of the main gate?"

"Well, bro," Sam started. "You scored two out of three. Yellow, I am not sure. It's more green from the algae on the walls. It stood deserted for almost two decades. But you seem to be familiar with that building."

"Not really. I happen to be travelling that way a lot. I've caught sight of the house on many occasions."

"So? What's your guess? How much would it cost?"

"I am not sure. But it's not gonna be below 6 crores," Pankaj stated absently.

"Woah! That's a huge amount," exclaimed Piyu.

Sam shrugged, "I didn't have any idea. But my uncle didn't sell it for some reason. That's why I, too, will not sell it right away. I will have to think before I take any decision."

"Hey, guys! Please excuse me. I'll meet you downstairs," Pankaj uttered and left oddly. Viren frowned clueless as he watched his brother take the stairs down.

"Anyways, what are we doing tomorrow?" Zac asked.

"I don't know. Viren and I will be working for most of the day," Sam started, "why don't you go with Piyu tomorrow and plan something to do in the evening. We will be free by five-ish."

"Who me?" asked a startled Zac.

"Sure," replied Piyu spontaneously. "Oh com'on Zacky boy, I am not gonna bite you," Piyu showed her canines like a lioness on the attack. "At least unless you make me," she added and winked.

After spending another hour, they left for the night. Viren made an offer to drop them at their respective places, which, looking at the hour, they readily accepted.

As soon as they left in Viren's car, three black SUVs rode past them in a hurry and screeched to stop right in front of the building Viren lived.

CHAPTER EIGHT

Delta Research Laboratory
Twenty Years Ago

Prof. Gowda entered his private office in DRL. He picked up the first mail from the pile on his desk, a fellowship request letter from an aspiring researcher. The second was an invoice for laboratory apparatuses from a local vendor.

He put the letters back on the desk and picked his voice recorder. He pressed and held the record button and started speaking in a monotonous, expressionless voice,

"August 19, 1992, IST 1848 hrs. Pre-clinical testing of candidate vaccine no. 79. Day 17 since exposure.

Test Subject 1. Species: Macaca Mulatta. Behaviour: slightly depressed; Viral load: constant; No disease progression.

Test Subject 2. Species: Macaca Mulatta. Behaviour: slightly depressed; Viral load: constant; No disease progression.

Test Subject 3. Species: Macaca Mulatta. Behaviour: slightly depressed; Viral load: constant; No disease progression.

Subjects 4, 5, and 6: preparing for exposure tomorrow."

He released the record button and put the recorder back on his desk. He picked the receiver of his desk phone and dialled a number. A few seconds later, his call got connected, "Hello Adhusudhan! How are you doing?"

"I am fine, Guru. How are you?" the man spoke on the other side of the phone.

"Great! There's some happy news?" Gowda said.

"About the vaccine?" Adhusudhan asked.

"Yes! I think it is working. The subjects are stable. There's no viral growth, and they seem as healthy as before infection. Today is the seventeenth day from the infection of the HIV-1 strain after vaccination from the recombinant HIV. It is the maximum any vaccine candidate has remained effective. Breaking the record of the previous one by fourteen days," Gowda spoke enthusiastically.

"That's great, my friend. I hope you succeed in your endeavour. Many lives will be saved by your discovery."

"Yes, I know. I also…" Gowda was stopped mid-sentence, a young man rushed into his office.

"Sir! You may want to see this," the man said. His fast-depleting hair pulled backwards.

"I'll talk to you later," the middle-aged researcher Gowda put the receiver down. He rose and followed the man.

"What has happened, Devdutt? Why are you so frenzied," Gowda shouted as he entered into the zoological section of the lab.

Devdutt pointed towards the three Asian apes inside the iron bar cages. He then pointed towards the biometric instruments that recorded their vitals.

"I'll be damned," Gowda uttered, rubbing his forehead.

Another man entered the lab. He had the highest authority. The man, who was called DK, stopped in his track beside Gowda and Devdutt. "Oh my god!" he uttered in astonishment.

CHAPTER NINE

Present Day

Following evening, Zac and Piyu met at the Café Coffee Day in Express Avenue, as suggested by Piyu. Zac took a cab and reached there to find Piyu sitting at a table for two. She wore black cotton shorts and a brilliant-blue off-shoulder top with a pair of black fish-mouthed bellies. She smiled and waved as she saw him enter the small coffee shop. He looked dashing in his white semi-transparent shirt and khaki pants. A pair of expensive Ray-Ban Laramie sunglasses dangled from the top button of his shirt.

They both ordered the same drink – chilling cold sparkle frappe with a scoop of vanilla ice-cream. After an hour of tattling, with Piyu doing most of the talking, they left the coffee shop and entered the nearby shopping mall. Piyu, like any other rich daddy's girl, loved shopping with or without any reason. Though today she had one, that being the month to be her last in India. She wanted to buy some farewell gifts for her friends in college, and a few for her mother, her father, and her two cousins.

An hour later, just as they moved out of the Lifestyle store inside the mall, someone called Piyu's name from behind. As they both turned, they found a young fair stunted boy in a skin-tight pink shirt and a red-brown cauterized pants, who jogged in their direction. Zac eyed the frail-looking boy from top to bottom. He was having a hard time resisting a chuckle at the bizarre fashion sense of the boy, who appeared to be some acquaintance of Piyu.

With a piercing through his lower lip and a clean-shaven face, he resembled some undistinguished gay American fashion designer.

"Oh, hey! Lucky!" she hugged him loosely just as he reached them. "What a surprise!"

"Not for me, really. If you had to find Piyu, you gotta look in a shopping mall," the gay-looking boy replied, placing his hands on her shoulders.

Piyu raised an eyebrow.

"Aah! Just kidding. B.T.W. Where the hell have you been lately? No see since the last exam," said the boy.

"Have been a little busy packing things up," she said. "Moving back to Melbourne, probably next month."

"What! Really?! What about Vishal? Is he okay with your decision?" he demanded.

"Actually….." Piyu pursed her lips.

"Oh my god! You guys broke up, didn't you?" he asked, genuinely surprised. He, like many others, had actually believed that Piyu and Vishal were meant for each other. They were so perfect together; nobody thought that they had been together for less than a year. "Are you guys still talking? Did it end well or just…" he added.

She shrugged and shook her head as she looked at Zac, who stood silently beside her hand-folded and expressionless.

"Well, it definitely came as a shock." He kept a hand on her shoulder and added, "Yet I believe, the almighty has kept special someone waiting for you, and you'll soon get what you deserve."

"Maybe or may not be. I still have a long career to work upon, and I don't want to lose my focus from that," she said and pursed her lips again. "By the way, this is Zac - Zac Wilson. A friend of mine from Melbourne," she turned to Zac, "and Zac, this is Lucky - my classmate and a very good friend of mine."

Zac extended a hand towards the short guy, "Hi!"

Lucky took a long moment to observe Zac, who stood towering above him with an awe-inspiring height of 6-1. He eyed Zac's silky brown hair deliberately in admiration. He shook his hand firmly and didn't leave before a long moment, just bordering on awkwardness.

Zac raised a brow, trying to gauge the intentions of the ill-looking boy. He gave him a hard look. *Fuck off, man! I'm not gonna be your date for tonight,* he said mutely.

The boy moved his gaze back to Piyu and said, "Why don't you come to my bro's party tonight. He is throwing a party for me, for I completed my MBA finally. I was going to call you anyway. It's a beach party. Here's the card," he handed her a small invitation card. "You got to be there," he paused for a moment, "And please bring your friend too," he eyed Zac.

"Sure. Meet you there then," she smiled.

"Okay then," he said and gave her a peck on the cheeks. "See you later," he added and turned to move away.

Piyu turned to Zac, "So…we got a place to hang out tonight. Let's take Sam and Viren along. Where are they?"

"I just got a text from Sam. They will be free in a quarter-hour. Where should I tell them to meet?" Zac demanded.

"This card says the party is 2 km south of the Marina Beach. We should meet at the Marina Beach. We will have more than 4 hours before the party starts," she suggested.

Zac punched on the virtual keypad of his I-phone 4S, relaying the message to Sam.

"There they are," Viren said, spotting Zac and Piyu idling on a rock at the beach. Viren and Sam walked towards them, reaching them from behind and tapping on Piyu's shoulder.

"Oh, hey! You are here," said Piyu.

"Finally," Zac added.

They walked along the stretch, killing time as much they could.

Piyu spotted a small make-shift tent at the back of the beach near the north end just south of the popular Marina Swimming Pool.

The board above the entrance of the tent announced, "Fortune Teller. Tarot Card Reading. Ask 3 questions for Rs. 100 only."

"Let's check it out. I've heard Tarot Card Reading actually works," Piyu said gleefully.

"I don't think so," Sam said, "I do believe in some of the superstitions, but this one is not among them."

"Not either me," Viren said, shaking his head. "In fact, I believe if we try to peek into the future, it alters, mostly, in an unpleasant way."

Piyu moved her gaze to Zac.

Zac felt a pressure building in his gut. Although, he too didn't believe in superstitions, yet he didn't wish to dishearten Piyu. "Hmm....I guess," Zac paused for a moment and continued, "What's the harm in trying?"

"Yes! Yes! Yes! What's the harm in trying? Well said, dude." She gave him a high-five.

After a few seconds, they found themselves standing inside the tent-house. Sam was still unsure of the whole thing and stood right at the threshold. He looked at the rustic middle-aged gypsy woman. She wore a thick eyeliner and a rosary bead tied around her forehead. There were three black dots in a triangle on her chin, which is called

'Drishti' and is put by rural people to ward-off negative energies. Her eyes bore into his deep as if she tried to hypnotize him and pull him towards herself. She spread a deck of precisely 78 tarot cards on the table, around a small glass sphere.

Piyu, Zac, and Viren asked questions in turns regarding their career, their love-life, and if they are going to be billionaires someday.

The gypsy woman moved her hands slowly and incessantly above the glass sphere as if drawing energy from it. She eyed the cards her clients drew and interpreted the meanings to them.

Piyu was told that everything she wanted in her life was standing right in front of her eyes. All she needed to do was open her eyes and grab it before it was too late.

Zac was told that patience was his greatest weapon. He would climb to the peak and get everything he wanted only if he would be patient.

Viren was told that struggle is what was written in most parts of his life. But hard work was the only oar he got to row his boat through the sea called 'life'.

"Come on, Sam. It's your turn now," Zac said.

"Nah! I'm fine," he waved his hand in refusal.

"Come, my child," the psychic said and nodded in assurance. "I know you have many questions in your mind. Just pour your heart out."

"No, thanks. I'm good."

"Come on, Sam, ask anything," Piyu snapped.

"Yeah, dude! Ask anything, whatever comes in your mind," said Zac.

After great persuasion, Sam finally agreed and moved towards the table. He looked at the woman into her eyes and asked, "I want to ask," he paused for a moment and continued, "Can I have more than one wife? I fantasize about having three wives. I know it's illegal in Australia, but can I?" he laughed out loudly, picked one card, and handed it to the psychic woman.

Piyu, Viren, and Zac stared at him blank-faced.

Sam turned back to his friends and said, "Sorry, guys, bad joke, I know. But I told you I don't believe in these types of nonsense. Let's go." He started walking back his way out.

"Let me ask you one question first. Do you know why you are here?" the gypsy woman asked eerily.

Sam and others turned back to find the woman standing face to face with Sam, she held up the card he had chosen for all of them to see. "Of course! I do," he replied.

"Life is never as it appears to be," she started. "There's always more than what meets the eyes. It's your destiny and karma that has brought you here. When your destiny unfolds itself, your life will never be like before. Someone or something close to you will be taken away. Many questions will be answered, many new ones will arise, and secrets will be revealed. You want to complete the work relegated to you, but you can do so only if you survive." She pulled his right hand up to look at it closely as she continued, "the obvious break in the lifeline of your palm indicates that you will be on crossroads where one way will take you towards life and another towards death. Everything will depend on the decision of yours and others around you."

Sam stood rooted at his place voiceless. Suddenly, he snatched his hand back from the woman, turned, and walked out of the tent. Piyu, Zac, and Viren followed.

"That damn bitch!" yelled Sam furiously.

After a long while, Sam was able to calm his nerves.

Later, they walked along the beach up to the party venue. There they danced, drank and danced with all their might.

Piyu didn't abate dancing even for a while and jumped over the sand with the beat crazily.

They got sloshed heavily and passed out one by one on the beach. Till they got their nerves back, it was already 6 in the morning. Zac woke up first and rubbed his eyes. He pressed his forehead with his fingers to soothe his aching head from the last night's hangover.

He turned rightwards to watch Piyu wincing from the sun's light falling on her eyes, still sleeping on the sand. On his left, he saw Viren and Sam still lying unconsciously. He turned his head about to find only a few people from last night's party still lying on the sand floor. Some of them slowly rising and moving their heads around groggily, trying to get their bearings back.

A thought, suddenly, crossed Zac's mind, and he frantically searched his trouser pockets. There was no purse, no mobile, nothing at all. *We are robbed.*

He nudged Sam violently and asked him to check his belongings. He was unable to find anything. In less than a minute, all four of them were wide awake and realized that they were robbed in the night while sleeping.

"Thank god, we did not have our passports with us," said Sam realizing that had they lost their passports, they would have been in a lot of trouble.

"We should report it to the police," Piyu suggested hazily, still coping with the hangover and pressing her forehead with her fingers.

"No, we can't. We have a flight to catch in six hours," Sam said. "I have a very important meeting in Melbourne tomorrow morning, and there's no flight later today. We have to move fast."

"Let Viren and I drop you at the airport then," Piyu offered.

"That will be great," Sam replied.

They scurried towards the road and took a cab for the hotel. As they entered the hotel, Sam stopped at the reception and asked the beautiful female receptionist to call a private car for the airport. He failed to notice that a man stood by the desk hiding his face behind a newspaper, waiting only for him. As soon as Sam left the desk for the elevator, the man folded his paper and moved out of the hotel.

One hour later, the quartet moved out of the hotel with two medium-sized suitcases. "Sir, your car is ready," declared the parking attendant.

They filled the car hastily, Viren sitting on the front passenger seat and the rest sitting at the back. The driver took his seat after placing the luggage in the boot-space of the Mahindra Xylo SUV and cranked up the engine.

"Driver, please hit the accelerator. We're in a little hurry," Sam pleaded when their car rode ridiculously slowly on an empty road.

"Mr. Samar Oza," said the driver, "I am afraid you are going to miss your flight." He hit the brakes hard on the deserted road, the vehicle screeched to stop. Before his passengers could comprehend what was happening, another SUV stopped beside them. Few men rushed out of the car and pointed guns at them. They quickly blindfolded the group and drove them through the early morning roads in the SUV with tinted windows.

CHAPTER TEN

Sam, Zac, Piyu, and Viren were dragged by the pack of goons. They were brought into a large sea-facing bungalow.

Sam tried to open his eyes but couldn't. He, as the other three, was blindfolded and his hands were tied behind his back. He wiggled his hands to slip through the knot. The more he tried to free his hands, the more they hurt bruising against the rough jute rope. Someone held him by his shoulders and pushed him down hard to make him collapse. Ready to hit against a hard floor, Sam, unexpectedly, fell onto a soft cushion. He realized that he was forced to sit on a sofa. He tried again with all his strength to break free from the bondage but to no avail. He turned his head left for the slightest input from his surroundings. Smoke entered his nose that smelled like some expensive cigar. He turned his head rightwards to hear the faint sound of sea waves breaking on the shore. *What place is this?*

"Where are we?" asked Viren. "Who are you people? And what do you want from us?" He felt a soft body leaning lightly against his right arm. He took in a faint musky scent of a ladies' perfume and instantly recognized it to be Piyu's.

"Viren! Are you okay? Where are Piyu and Zac?" asked Sam.

"I am here too," replied Piyu.

Sam instantly located the source of the voice. It came from the same direction as of Viren's - right in front of him.

"Sam, it's me here," Zac said and nudged Sam from left.

"See guys," Sam said, now addressing their captors, "if you want money. Just tell me the number and get over with all the drama."

There was no response.

"Just tell me what your demands are?" Sam said again. In the silence, he could hear the thumping of his heart against his chest. "Come on, give it a voice, damn it," he yelled.

"I don't think anybody's here," whispered Zac.

"Shhh! There is someone. I can smell smoke. Probably a cigar," said Sam in a low tone, raising his nose slightly to locate the source of the smell. "They are watching us," he added.

There was a sudden loud sound of applause from a single pair of hands.

"Amazing!" a deep airy voice of a man said. The voice sounded to be of someone well past his youth and passing through his early old age. "As the son, as the father," the voice said again.

Suddenly, without warning, Sam found his eyes unblinded. He tried to open his eyes and closed it reflexively. His eyes now adapted to the dark of the blindfold took a moment to adjust for the bright day-light background. One-by-one, Zac, Piyu, and Viren also got unblinded by some forceful, confident, and unshaken hands.

Their eyes struggled to adjust to their bright surroundings. Almost together, they saw each other. They found themselves sitting on two small low-height couches, covered in pure-white velvet fabric. The two couches faced each-other, separated by a low glass-top rectangular table. Piyu and Viren sat on one couch, and on the other sat Zac and Sam.

Sam turned left to see an old man sitting on a couch built for one. He had a dark complexion, average height, and a stout frame with a little paunch. He wore a well-tailored shirt made with expensive off-white poplin fabric and dark brown pants.

He jerked the cigar on the ashtray placed over the glass-top corner table on his right. He held his cigar outwards between his right index and middle fingers and scratched his forehead with his ring finger. His head was full of grey short curly hair, without even a trace of baldness, unlike many of his age. He lowered his hand and took a long drag from his Cuban cigar. Its band spelt Trinidad.

Another man middle-aged, tall, dark, and muscular with heavily bearded face stood behind him at his left, with his arms folded over his chest. He was clothed in a tight-fitting black t-shirt with a picture of a screaming skull on its front. Three long gold chains dangled on his neck. His shabby black cargo pants looked little out of place. There was nobody else in the room except the six of them.

Sam eyed the old man for a long moment before he asked harshly, "What do you want? And how do you know my father?"

"Relax, young man. I know you have many questions," the old man said and paused for a drag. "Some questions take a long time to get answered. Even I have been waiting for twenty long years with many unanswered questions."

Sam narrowed his eyes, apparently having a hard time contemplating the intentions of this old man. He tried hard to remember if he saw this man anytime in his childhood.

"Don't try so hard," the old man started, "I know you don't know me. But I know you well. I have been looking for you ever since you flew out of the country with your uncle. I still can't believe that you have been hiding from me for more than twenty years."

This man has been looking for me for twenty years? What does he want so badly from me?

"Even I don't believe that you've been looking for me for such a long time," said Sam.

"Believe it or not, but you can prove to be a very precious asset for me," said the old man as he shoved his cigar into the ashtray.

"I don't want to prove to be anything to you. Just let me and my friends go *right now*," Sam said in a high tone with a sense of least felt fearlessness.

The old man gave the nod to the man behind him.

The man came forward and fished out a large folding knife with a wooden folder. He lunged towards Piyu, who instantly jerked backwards and leaned harder on Viren. The man held her by her hands and swiped the knife in a slicing motion against the rope, smoothly cutting the knot. He, then, lunged towards Viren and untied his hands too. He continued until he freed all four of them.

"My friends! Don't take me wrong. Consider me your well-wisher. I am working for a noble cause for the benefit of society. My name is Dr. Daanish Kandiyar, or you can call me DK."

The four looked at each other incomprehensively.

DK continued, "I know my way of conduct is wrong. Many people have been complaining about it." He smirked. "But a proper end justifies all means, doesn't it Mr. Samar Oza?"

"And what that proper end might be? Can we dare to ask?" asked Sam.

"Your answers are coming well-personified, young man. You will be offered all the explanations. All you have to do is wait for the right moment. Be my guest; see yourselves to the bar," DK motioned with his hand showing the way to the bar, "but please don't try to leave the premises. Any inconvenience caused is highly regretted."

"I have to use the loo," stated Piyu, her expressions showing a hint of desperation.

"Ah! The classic women-and-the-loo problem. Rajan!" he addressed to his man, "please see my lady to the washroom. She is our guest and should be treated as one by all means."

The muscular middle-aged man nodded promptly.

An hour had passed. Sam and his friends were being worried. They had simulated various possibilities that could happen in their minds. It gave the feeling of agitation and anger, along with fear. They had already lost their mobiles and wallets. Now, their luggage was also taken away from them.

They cogitated about any potential escape route, but nothing seemed promising. They knew very well that they were held hostages, and the situation could turn hostile any minute. They had to keep their calm and try not to aggravate it.

Sam eyed the tall, muscular dark man in the skull-print t-shirt. He stood deathly still most of the time behind Viren's and Piyu's back, except on occasions when his phone rang, and he moved a few steps away to answer it.

Viren fathomed the idea of attacking the man as the odds were in favour of them by three-and-a-half by one. But he decided against since he had no idea how many more would be waiting outside the gates of the bungalow. Moreover, he had already spotted two close circuit cameras at the two corners of the large hall. Their status LEDs glowed dimly red, leaving no doubt that they were operational.

More time passed before they finally watched DK entering the hall from the main entrance, being followed by a suited man. The new entrant looked pale, his head going bald with age. His fast thinning hairs were yet black and pulled backwards, pasted with oil. His wrinkled face and dark circles under his eyes made him look sixty, though he was a little over fifty. He wore a grey suit and carried a black briefcase.

Both men neared the sitting area, where Sam and his friends sat for the last couple of hours. They stood up seeing the men closing in, hoping that their ordeal was over and they could leave now. Though it was far from the truth.

DK stopped beside his man Rajan and folded his hands as a sign of having his part done. The other man continued till he reached the single sofa where DK sat earlier. He looked at all four of them and said, "Hello Mr. Samar Oza," as he extended his arm directly towards Sam. "It's been a very long time, twenty long years to be precise."

Sam frowned. His eyes narrowed and gave a hard look. He refused to shake hands with one of his captors.

"Very well," the man took his hand back. "Since you may not remember me, I should introduce myself to you first. My name is Dr. Devdutt, senior research scientist National AIDS Research Institute, Pune."

The quartet frowned, hearing the word AIDS.

Sam wondered what a research scientist from an AIDS research centre could possibly want from him.

"I ought to tell you, you have your mother's eyes. She had one angelic pair of them. And your nose is just like your father Jaswant – broad and round," the man said, a broad smile stuck on his face.

"See, Doctor," Sam replied crisply. "I have no idea who you are. Even if we had met when my parents were still part of this world, that must have been twenty years ago when I was just five. It would be easy for all of us if you can skip straight to the point and tell me what you want from me."

"Alright," Devdutt said, his face turned straight, "Let's skip to the point." He gestured for them to take their respective seats and sat down himself. Everyone followed. He continued, "We only want a small help from you, and we will be very obliged if you cooperate."

"Why should I help you?" asked Sam.

"Because helping us would mean helping your father fulfil his last wish."

Sam waited for a minute before asking, "what kind of help?"

"You have something, we believe, in your possession. We want that from you. That's all."

"What that thing might be, dare I ask? And what was my father's last wish that you want to fulfil more than I do?"

"I don't think it's under your domain of expertise to understand all of this," Devdutt said and paused to look at DK "But we want you to trust us," he added.

"See sir, it's not before I understand the whole story that I'll decide whether to help you or not," Sam replied bitterly.

Zac, Piyu, and Viren sat in confusion, yet to decide their role in the ploy.

"Very well," he said as he moved his gaze towards DK, who gave a slight nod in consent. "What do you know about HIV?" the scientist asked.

"Only that you never want to cross its path if you want to live. Causes AIDS, transferred by unprotected sexual contact or blood transfusion from an infected person," Sam replied, hoping that's what the man wanted to hear.

"Hmm….that may be the gist of it. Do you have any knowledge in microbiology, specifically molecular virology?"

"I have some of it," Zac intervened. "I have a medical background, and I have read various books."

"That's great. Can you please testify what I am about to say. Your friend may believe you more than he will believe me."

Zac gave an irresolute nod.

"Have you heard of Prof. Gurudutt Gowda? He was a very good friend of your father. Maybe your uncle had told you about him if he ever talked about your parents," he asked.

"Only the name. My uncle had shown his photo once from my birthday album. Nothing remarkable he told me about him," Sam replied.

"Alright. For starter, Prof. Gurudutt Gowda was a brilliant scientist, researcher, and academician. He had made many breakthroughs in the domain of Microbiology. Sadly, he died an untimely and suspicious death."

"Prof. Gowda," the man continued, "used to work for Delta Research Laboratory, Chennai. DRL, which works in collaboration with Vladimir Research Laboratory, Russia, and is managed by Dr. Khandiyar," he motioned his hand towards DK. "He also taught in the IIT Madras as an adjunct professor. Gowda was conducting research on a pre-infection treatment for HIV. Gowda was an extraordinary researcher, who miraculously found a preventive measure against HIV which could save millions of lives – a miracle yet to be performed by our scientists even twenty years later."

"How had he actually managed to do so?" demanded Zac.

"To understand that you have to first understand what HIV is and how does it work. I should try to explain it going least technical about it and without entering into the details," the pasty looking scientist said. Sam nodded in acknowledgement. "HIV is a type of retrovirus. Retroviruses are those who have RNA but no DNA. Once they infect a cell, they convert their RNA into DNA by the use of enzymes. Once their DNA is formed, it is integrated into the cell's own DNA and becomes provirus. There it sits idly for a long time," the scientist paused for a moment for the information to settle into the minds of his young listeners. He continued, "Once the cell becomes active, the DNA of the virus is replicated by the cell's own replication process. After that, a specific enzyme reads from the DNA of the virus and manufactures the proteins required for the formation of a whole new virus particle, which later leaves the cell taking some of its outer membrane, thus completing a cycle."

Zac nodded as a curious student. Sam, Piyu, and Viren tried to understand the concept, at least partially, if not wholly.

"One of the major characteristics of HIV is that it only infects a certain type of cells called T-helper cells which carry a special protein CD4+, without which there can be no entry for the virus into the cell. T-helper cells are an essential part of the Human Immune System. Moreover, HIV can't stay for a long time in the air. That's why it can be communicated only through bodily fluids such as blood, semen, vaginal fluids, et cetera. Had it been an air-borne virus, HIV would have become the cause of human extinction."

"And what Prof. Gowda did to protect our immune cells from this killer virus?" Piyu asked, genuinely intrigued by the information.

The man smiled and said, "he somehow managed to isolate strains of the HIV-1 virus, which is the more common type. He used complex Recombinant DNA techniques to alter the genetic structure of the virus. Scientists have used this technique many times to create Recombinant Viruses for various purposes. There even has been researches to put these Viruses in use to prevent or cure cancer. HIV has a rather simpler genetic structure. It has only nine genes as compared to a thousand in bacteria and about an average of twenty-four thousand in human beings."

"So what Prof. Gowda did was - use these Recombinant HIVs to fight real lethal HIVs," said Sam.

"More or less so. HIV has certain p24 proteins, which act as antigen and reacts with the T-helper cells, thus, triggering its destruction. It continues to do so until the count of these T-helper cells drops below a minimum limit - 200 cells per microliter to be precise - and the person acquires AIDS. So what Gowda actually did was – he altered some of the genes of HIV-1 to alter its functionality, especially its production of p24 protein by the process called gene expression. He made it a harmless version of the actual HIV. Thus, in its essence, this friendly HIV infects a human body in a way similar to the killer HIV. But rather than killing the cells, it sits inside it idly. These types of viruses are called stealth virus."

Zac scrutinized each and every word the man said. "It means even if you are infected with HIV, you still don't die?" he asked, "But what will happen if an actual killer-HIV infects the person?"

"If an actual HIV infects a cell which is already infected by our friendly HIV, co-infection will occur. Co-infection often occurs with HIV, especially with tuberculosis in later stages of HIV infection. In some countries, 80% of tuberculosis patients are also infected with HIV. Gowda designed the Recombinant Virus in such a way that it will suppress the genes of the killer HIV, thus, preventing the manufacture of its proteins. Without completing the cycle, HIV will die with the few cells infected by it, and there will be no or less propagation of the disease. Although it did not guarantee complete protection from HIV, it ensured slow progression delaying death by at least two to three decades. It is in addition to the fifteen to twenty years added by the modern anti-retroviral drugs. It is enough time for an adult person to lead his complete lifespan and die naturally. Ask the person suffering from cancer who undergoes excruciating radiotherapy to delay his death by only two to three years."

Sam nodded in acceptance.

"That's really impressive," said Viren after a long time. "But I am wondering if you already know the process, what stops you from making this thing happen?"

"This is the problem with science. Things are easier said than done. In this respect, we have been trying to study the genetic structure of the virus for a long time now. But altering it to make the virus perform according to our will can be a little tricky. In some attempts, the modified virus became so weak that it could not even infiltrate the cell and died in the process. Lately, we have made it infiltrate, but it could not stay idle for a long time. It rapidly mutated and ultimately killed the cell. HIVs are the fastest evolving entities known to man. That's why the treatment of HIV involves frequent changes in drugs. Each time a new drug is prescribed to a patient, the virus evolves and becomes immune to that drug, thus, requiring a new class of drugs after every couple of years. Nowadays, medical practitioners prescribe three different classes of drugs to the patient simultaneously. But this weakens the individual greatly and disrupts his metabolism."

"But if Gowda had already done it and he worked for you people? Why didn't he give it to you?" asked Viren again.

"He didn't need to give it to us. He had signed a contract with Delta Research Lab, which mandated that any discovery made by him while working in DRL will be owned by DRL. But we never denied him the credit he deserved. We also offered him handsome royalty," Devdutt said.

"Then, why are you empty-handed even after twenty years?" Viren smirked.

"That's because Gowda fell victim to his greed. He wanted to make most out of his discovery. He even approached a South Korean company to sell his research. That would have meant monopoly of the treatment, and this type of treatment that ensured a cure against an otherwise incurable fatal disease would be sold in millions of dollars to the creamy layer of the population. Thus, India would have to import the vaccine making it impossible for the poor, needy Indian people to afford it. We admit we too were not completely driven by patriotism, but our goals involved benefits for our country also."

"What happened to the research, then?" asked Sam.

"We came to know that Gowda had started pre-clinical animal trials without clearance from the authorities. He was desperate to prove his research to the Koreans. When we confronted him about this, he destroyed the samples he had made and sheltered his notes with your father, who was his childhood friend. We threatened him to sue him in court. In response, he threatened us to destroy the findings. He said it was all in his mind, and we could not make him talk by any means. We had believed he was bluffing, that's why we called his bluff. But he really asked your father to destroy his notes."

"That's where you lost the cause," uttered Sam.

"No. Not there. Your father, Jaswant Oza, was a smart man. He was an inventor and a visionary too. He maintained his neutrality and was ready to betray his friend for the larger good. But he did not trust us either."

"But what he had to do with it? As far as I know, he was a polymer scientist, not a microbiologist," asked Sam.

"Indeed, he was a polymer scientist and a nanotechnologist, and an *excellent* one too. He worked at IIT Madras earlier. He had named few patents for his developments in biodegradable plastics. He acted smartly by not obliterating the research of Gowda but sealed it in an almost impenetrable package." Devdutt nodded to DK, who moved promptly towards the farthest side of the hall.

He approached a small open area near the staircase at the northwest corner. He looked at a broad picture of an Andalusian horse, whose front legs were raised high in the air, ready to sprint. There was no saddle on the horse. There was a fence in front of it, and it was all determined to cross over the fence.

DK rotated the picture anti-clockwise to reveal a small electronic locker behind it embedded into the wall. He quickly entered the numeric code and removed a smaller locker from its inside. This smaller locker had a combination lock with a dialler mechanism. DK quickly closed the larger locker and replaced the picture to its original position. He carried the smaller locker back with him.

"It does not appear to be as impenetrable as you claimed it to be," Piyu uttered.

Nobody offered an explanation.

DK placed the locker on the rectangular glass-top table and started rotating the dials to open it. It opened with a click. Devdutt bent down and precariously removed a 30cmx20cmx12cm thermocol box with his both hands. He placed it carefully over the locker. He then pulled the top half with his hands to reveal a large mass of raw cotton. He started slowly tearing off the cotton from the top until a red package appeared. He picked up the red package slowly and carefully and handed it over to Devdutt with utmost care.

"This is the almost impenetrable packaging you were talking about?" asked Zac.

"Don't judge a book by its cover, my child. This idiom suits this thing perfectly."

Piyu, Viren, Zac, and Sam leaned in to watch the object closely. It didn't look like anything more than a well-packed birthday present wrapped in a cheap gift paper. It had a lustrous blood-red surface with a smooth, glossy texture like a snooker ball. Sam was intrigued because he noticed that the package was seamless. Then, how did its content reached inside it? Soon he realized that the covering was some kind of plastic that was poured over its content in a molten state.

"As you may have already concluded that this is a plastic which covered its contents to protect them from damage," asked Devdutt.

Everyone nodded.

"But this is not the case. In fact, it is designed to destroy its contents if there is an attempt to break the seal."

The quartet awed in surprise and leaned closer to scrutinize the object more closely.

"This covering," the man continued, "is a scientifically designed material. All we know about it is that this thing is highly sensitive. It contains nitroglycerine suspended in a cross-linked polymer that explodes by the slightest shock or heating. A single crack in its surface will result in an explosion."

Untold to anyone in the world, Sam's father had designed a mixture of sensitized nitroglycerine suspended in a matrix of an inorganic polymer and animal protein. It had a complimentary solution which, when mixed together, will make it hard as a rock, similar to the patented adhesive Araldite, but by changing the structure of the protein rather than undergoing chemical reactions. This hardened polymer was but a single giant molecule of cross-linked polymer, like a tire which is a single polymeric molecule of rubber cross-linked with sulphur molecules in a process called vulcanization. In the case of a crack in the compound, a slight mechanical shock would be released at the molecular level, which was sufficient to start a chain explosion of nitroglycerine.

This whole process is done at sub-zero temperatures. Another protective layer of thermosetting plastic is moulded below the ignition-temperature of nitroglycerine of 218ºC. It prevents the explosion of nitroglycerine at room temperature. This is what gave the lustrous, smooth texture to the surface of the package.

Devdutt watched his audience lost deep in thoughts. He continued, "It can be opened in only one way. Jaswant made another solution which can dissolve this covering without damaging its contents."

"There's another way. Can't we disintegrate the surface under deoxygenated water or in a vacuum," Viren suggested.

The scientist gave it a thought for a moment and then replied, "No use. Nitro glycerine is a self-oxidizing fuel. It carries its own oxidant and doesn't need any extra oxygen from outside. It would be very risky to try anything at all to break this open forcefully. This thing carries lifesaving capability for millions."

"What if we freeze it to very low temperature? Isn't it called desensitization of nitroglycerine, which is used for its transportation?" Viren suggested again, though, from an IT background, he had a keen interest in reading online scientific journals while in college.

"Yes, it is. But the explosive material is suspended in a cross-linked polymer. There will be molecular forces acting within. Breaking this open means breaking molecular bonds. Molecular bonds break with a release of energy that disturbs the nitroglycerine, thus, bringing us back to the square one. As I have already told you, this is very risky, and stakes are really high. If there's any way it can be opened is with the solution, which, we believe lies within your possession," Devdutt fixed his gaze on Sam.

Sam sat in silence for a long time. He stared at the red package lying in front of him and tried to process all the information he had just heard. "You said you want to fulfil my father's last wish," he said finally. "What was his last wish?"

"Your father did not destroy the research for an excellent reason. He wanted the whole society to benefit from it. But he did not know whom to trust. That's why he locked it for some time for the dust to settle. But that was his biggest mistake. He formed a long line of enemies after him. Things turned dirty, and he lost his life before he could give the key to anyone."

"Are you suggesting that my parents did not die in an accident but were murdered?" asked Sam.

"I am not suggesting *anything,* but I do not completely deny the idea. The Koreans can be very offensive," said Devdutt.

Sam stood up and slowly walked to face the sea. He waited for a long moment before he said, "You mean there is at least a possibility that my father might have been murdered."

"A slight possibility," said the scientist.

"And you said he made a long line of enemies."

"That's true."

"Then, isn't there a slight possibility that *you* might have murdered him as well?" Sam turned to face DK and Devdutt. "Weren't you his enemy too?"

CHAPTER ELEVEN

Sam and his friends were moved to a large bedroom on the first floor of the bungalow. The room was painted in saffron with white ceilings. There was a large bed lying in the middle of the longer wall facing right against the door.

Ten hours had passed since they were taken hostages. It was early in the evening, and the summer sun glowed like a giant red ball in the western sky just above the horizon.

Piyu stood by the large ceiling-to-floor glass door of the balcony looking at the calm sea. She spotted five unruly men in torn-off clothes sitting on the sand and playing cards. She could see a gun lying beside one of them.

Zac and Viren sat on the bed, resting their back against the head of the bed. Viren folded his hands and was lost deep in his thoughts, fathoming the recent turn of events.

Sam sat on the easy chair and looked through the glass door into the sky.

DK, Devdutt, and Rajan entered the room. Zac and Viren straightened their back. Sam rose from the chair as Piyu turned to the door.

"Have you made your decision? Or shall we start our next phase of extracting information from you?" DK smirked. He brushed a small wooden showcase lying at the corner with his finger and picked some dirt. "I hope you like this place as you might be staying for a little while here. This room hasn't been occupied by any soul for a long time."

"I remember now," Samar said. "I was here, in this place, all those years ago."

Zac and Viren looked at each other.

DK smiled. "That's good. Now think harder. I want that solution."

"See. I have told you I don't have a solution of any sort that you might be seeking. My father may have sealed those notes, but its keys he didn't leave with me. And moreover, why would I help my father's murderer?" said Sam.

"Errrr! That was a wrong answer. For this, you will be penalized," DK said signalling his man Rajan.

Rajan moved towards Piyu. He held her arm and started dragging her towards DK

Piyu rebuked forcefully. "Leave me, you dirty shit of a fish," she yelled.

Sam came forward and freed her from the goon's hands. Zac and Viren also stood up.

"I know you have all the reasons to take us as your parents' killer. But you still have many others whom you may not want to lose. Moreover, it will be no good to your deceased parents if you're dead. Your father made a mistake by keeping that vaccine from the world. You should not repeat the mistakes of your father," DK said.

"Fine. I'm ready to give you whatever the hell you want," Sam said. "But still, I don't have the solution."

"Then put some more load on your memory. There *is* a key to open the seal, and it's only you whom Jaswant could trust that with. He even managed to keep you hidden from us for twenty years. We couldn't have imagined that you had been flown out to as far as Australia if you hadn't come back."

Sam stared silently.

"I give you fourteen hours. A flight ticket is booked for you for tomorrow morning and a return ticket for tomorrow night. Rajan will escort you. Your friends will remain our guests until you give us the solution. If there's any detour from the plan, the fishes will be more than happy to have your friends on dinner," the old man said.

"I think I know what you need. It's not exactly what you are asking for. But I am sure you will be happy to have it," said Sam.

"What's it?"

"A package the same as you showed us earlier."

"What?! Were you able to open it?" asked DK as he scratched his forehead with a finger.

"My uncle showed it to me in his locker and asked not to open it ever. He just wanted me to know that it exists." Sam remembered the day. His uncle was recently diagnosed with acoustic neuroma, a type of brain tumour. The tumour had been developing inside his brain for over a year at a slow pace. It was not until he faced some hearing problems that he consulted an ENT specialist, who further referred him to a neurosurgeon. The neurosurgeon immediately recommended surgical removal of the tumour. He had also warned the high failure rate of the surgery and the development of dementia and incontinence upon survival. That's why Naresh Mehrotra, Sam's uncle, transferred the ownership of the locker to Sam and handed its key to him. Fatefully, he had survived the surgery only to live for another six months before which his tumour had turned malignant and incurable. Finally, he succumbed to his pains, leaving Sam as the heir of his legacy Mehrotra Export & Import.

"What that could be?" DK wondered.

"I know what it is," Devdutt butted in. "It's the formula for the seal itself. Jaswant had sealed his own discovery too. He believed once the vaccine is unsealed and put to use by people with good motives, his formula could be used as a communication method by the military or the intelligence," he said. "It must contain the formula of the solution to break the seal also."

"But how shall we open that one, without the solution itself?" asked DK

"I don't know for sure. But this is a lead we must follow unless we are too insane," Devdutt suggested.

Next Day, Melbourne

Sam flagged down a taxi and took it directly to his bungalow in the suburbs of Heidelberg Heights. There he collected a small key from his locker and drove his car to a privately owned vault facility at William Street, few kilometres drive from his house.

After following a long security protocol of logging the entry electronically into the computer and proving his identity with a biometric hand scanner and digital photo recognition, he was allowed to enter the vault area along with Rajan. He fished out his key and inserted it through the keyhole. He rotated the key a whole circle, and the locker opened with a click. He un-shut the door of the locker and pulled out a cuboidal 50cm x 25cm x 15cm safety box made up of prime quality tested steel and coated with high-quality corrosion-resistant enamel paint.

A small brass handle protruded from the top face near one of the ends of the longer side. Sam pulled the handle halfway backwards to reveal a glazy ultramarine-blue coloured package, much like the red one in DK's possession; only it was smaller about three-quarters of the other one. The deposit box was ridiculously oversized to host the single 22cm x 15cm x 8cm cuboidal package.

Samar removed the package carefully from the locker and placed it over the bench. He eyed again into the box only to find a cylindrical tool about half-foot long and one-inch in diameter. He took the tool out of the box and placed it adjacent to the blue package.

Samar held the cylinder close to his face and scrutinized it from all angles. It was a silvery grey piece of metal, probably made up of aluminium alloy. On closer inspection, he realized it was not a true cylinder but decagonal in cross-section with ten longitudinal faces and filleted edges. On one of its faces, it had seven circular dials with numbers from 0 to 9 engraved on each of them circumferentially. It had a large hole in one of its cross-sectional face and a push-button on the opposite. He pushed the button down, but to no use. It took no longer for him to recognize it to be a Dial Combination Lock, with one million possible combinations. But lock for what? It didn't seem to be containing anything.

Rajan picked the package from the bench and snatched the lock away from Samar's hands. On exiting the premises, Rajan took out some bubble wraps from his shoulder bag. He carefully wrapped the bubble wraps around the blue package in three layers and placed it inside his bag.

They drove to the airport directly and took the very next flight back to Chennai, which was not until midnight.

CHAPTER TWELVE

Viren sat on the sofa chair in the bedroom. It was a new morning, and the sun had just risen. It had been close to seventy-two hours that he, Zac, and Piyu were held captive in the house. He hadn't slept for even a single moment in that whole time.

He watched Zac slightly dozing off at the right side of the bed, supporting his back against the head of it. He moved his gaze to Piyu, who slept peacefully and assumed a fetal position facing Zac, on the left side of the bed. Her bare slender legs below her thigh-length black shorts glistened in the early morning sunlight peeping through the window. Her blue off-shoulder top rose slightly to reveal her fair, narrow waist. Her skin was soft and flawless. Viren admired her slim, hourglass figure for a long moment. He jerked his head and looked away through the window.

The sun slowly rose higher in the sky. Its rays filling the room gradually until it reached Zac's face, who winced by the sudden brightness and came out of sleep with a start. He noticed Piyu still lost in her dreams. He eyed Viren, who looked towards the sea, lost in his thoughts.

Without warning, the door opened, and a dark rustic thug-like man came into the room. "Come on," he said, "you are summoned downstairs." He looked at napping Piyu from top to bottom evil-eyed, then looked at Zac, who gave him a hard look and turned to make his way back to where he had come from.

A few minutes later, Viren, along with Zac and Piyu, climbed down the stairs into the antechamber on the ground floor. They were more than happy to see Samar sitting on the sofa. DK sat on his usual single sofa chair. Rajan stood, as usual, behind him to his left. Devdutt, however, was nowhere to be seen.

"Are you guys alright?" asked Sam upon their arrival.

All three of them nodded tenderly.

"Now, you have everything we had to offer you," Samar said, "please let me and my friends go."

DK was so lost in scrutinizing the new blue package and the slender piece of metal with the dials, he hardly heard the young man.

"Let us go, dammit. It's enough of enough," Samar shouted and banged his fist on the glass-top table.

Rajan put a step forwards but was stopped by DK He looked at Samar narrow-eyed. He was about to say something when suddenly five men barged into the bungalow through the main entrance. They looked uncivilized, repulsive people, and walked right close to where Rajan was standing. DK turned his head and stood up promptly.

One of the men came forward as the others stood behind him. He was pale, in his middle-aged, and had light brown hair pulled backwards. He wore a brown leather-look blazer, which looked preposterously inappropriate given the time of the year. His freckled skin and green-grey eyes gave out his Russian ethnicity. It was evident that he was coming directly from Russia, probably northern parts, as he was yet to notice the hotter climate of India as compared to that of his country.

"Leonid! What are you doing here?" asked DK, surprised.

"Vladimir has sent me," said the man in Russian, "he wants to talk to you, yet you seem to be audacious enough to ignore his calls. He has sent me to take you to him myself."

"I know there had been some issues. Trust me, it was not my fault at all. I had ensured everything was according to the plan; it seems there is some leak in our circle," DK said solemnly in Russian.

"Some issues?! You call it just some issues?!" Leonid caught DK by his collars and continued, "You have made a loss of two hundred million rubbles to us, about forty crores in that of your puny currency. Who is gonna pay that sum back? You?"

"Yes, I will. I will pay double of what I owe you, only if you give me some time."

Leonid laughed out loud and let the man's collar go. "You talk about double? I will leave you for half. But I want the money *right now.*"

"Right now? How shall I get that much amount right now," DK said as he placed his left hand on his waist and ran his right hand through his hair. "You *have* to give me some time."

"For that, you have to come with me, and Vladimir will, himself, decide what has to be done with you," Leonid said with an air of finality.

"What if I refuse?"

The Russian looked directly into the old man's aging eyes for a full minute before he gestured his men with his head.

DK stepped backwards and pulled out a 9mm Beretta semi-automatic pistol. Rajan followed suit. The Russian and his men also pulled out their pistols.

Sam and his friends got closer to each other and took several steps away from them.

The Russian man pointed his gun directly at DK's face. "I didn't want it to be this way," he smirked. He knew he outnumbered DK by five to two.

Soon, four more men rushed into the hall through the beach-faced glass door and stood beside DK

Samar, Zac, Viren, and Piyu ran and crouched behind the bar. Without warning, two bullets were fired. Samar raised his head slightly above the bar to see two men lying on the floor and others hiding behind different things ranging from the columns of the building to the sofa where Sam sat a few minutes ago to a small partition wall at one corner. Another bullet was fired, but it missed Rajan closely. He fired back, and one of the Russian men got hit on the chest and fell onto the floor. The next minute, bullets were fired continuously from both sides. There were four men surviving - the Russian and one of his men on one side and DK and Rajan on the other.

Samar turned his head right and looked at the wide-open glass door opening to the beach. It was their only chance of escape, and he didn't wish to miss it. He crouched back and explained the situation to his friends. He told them to run as fast as possible out of that door. They crawled slowly towards the door to get as close to it under cover of the bar desk. There they stood up and ran as fast as possible, letting Piyu run before them, followed by Viren, Samar, and Zac. They smoothly got out through the door and ran towards the sea. Samar turned back to check on Zac, but he was not there. He stopped and ran back to get his friend.

Zac had stopped just at the threshold and ran back to the sofa and took the blue package and the metal tool. DK looked mockingly at the boy braving such an attempt amidst all the chaos. He pointed his gun towards Zac and fired. The bullet missed Zac's neck only by few inches. The Russian man fired at DK, who also got saved by inches. Zac strode fast, taking big steps with his long stout legs and got through the door. He was caught by Samar, who was just going in looking for his childhood friend. On finding him unscathed, Samar ran fast towards the sea where Viren and Piyu stood waiting for them, followed by Zac. They ran along the shore northwards until they hit the road again. There, they hired a cab and commanded the driver to drive speedily without giving any proper destination.

"What's wrong with you man," Samar yelled at Zac, "Why did you have to bring this thing with you?" he pointed to the blue package in Zac's hands that he risked his life for.

Samar and his friends travelled in the cab from one direction to another for half an hour, to make sure nobody followed their trail. Viren was sitting on the front seat beside the driver, and Samar sat between Zac and Piyu at the back.

Zac looked at the blue package in one of his hands and the metal tool in the other. He had valiantly rescued the items amidst the totally hostile situation. He looked at Samar and uttered in his thick Australian accent, "Sam! This thing has been left by your father for you. This is the only thing you have with yourself which had ever been touched by your parents." He watched Samar's eyes shot red in anger but continued, "I didn't want you to lose your parents' last belonging."

Sam kept silent. He knew Zac would never do anything with poor intentions. He was furious because Zac had endangered his own life for a pretty mundane object which held no value to him. Even if there was a key to open the seal which contained a valuable vaccine, Sam didn't want to make any claim on it, especially, if it meant putting his and his friends' life in harm's way. He would simply let DK take the vaccine and name all the credits of it.

"And just think about this," Zac said, "If your father didn't want to give this vaccine to DK, he must have had some reasons. He even has possibly lost his life protecting this thing. Who knows if it was DK who was after all responsible for your parents' demise? I feel you should respect your father's decision and go to the very core of the matter first."

"One thing I don't understand," Viren said, "A man as DK, with so many resources; How on earth couldn't he trace you in twenty years? How did you manage to evade him for such a long time that too unwittingly?"

"I know how," said Samar absently.

"How?"

"That's because 'Samar' has not always been my name."

"What!" Zac exclaimed.

"Yes. My name was used to be Naman Oza. My uncle changed it when he took me with him. Now I know why. Since I was still a kid then, it didn't take much of paperwork. My identity changed from Naman to Samar, almost overnight."

"But what should we do now?" Zac demanded.

"I think we should go to the police," Viren suggested.

The cab stopped on the side of a busy road. Samar stood behind it. He looked across the street. *A police station*. He looked back at his friends. Piyu nodded, "We are with you," she said.

Samar had taken just a step forward that a car rode fast from the wrong side and screeched to stop right in front of him. A long black sedan - luxurious and expensive. The driver shoved out a .38 caliber revolver and pointed directly at Samar's guts. He was an old man, probably a sexagenarian. He wore a full-sleeves black shirt, hair mostly grey but covered his head entirely. His red-brown thick full-rim eyeglasses with photo-chromatic lenses were modern-ish and deceived his age. His salt-pepper French cut beard displayed an undying spark in him. But his wrinkled face and palm gave away enough.

Viren tried to run and reach the police station fast.

"I'll make so many holes in this poor bastard friend of yours," the driver said, "you'll never be able to count all of them."

The confidence and ruthlessness in his voice made Viren stop in his tracks. He looked at Samar's face and then at the gun.

"He's bluffing. He cannot kill me here in public," Samar yelled.

"I don't have anything to lose, I have already lived enough. And moreover, before even will any one of you be able to speak, this baby of mine will take me miles away from here." He pointed to his car.

"What do you want?" asked Samar.

"Please sit in the car," the man said, "All of you."

DK flipped the dead body of the Russian mafia lord Leonid with his foot. There were three bullet holes in his chest. Two were in the lower abdominal that didn't seem fatal as much as the one in the middle of his ribs, right through the heart.

He looked all around the house and found nine dead bodies. All the men with the Russian had died along with the four of DK's men. DK and Rajan were the lone survivors.

He motioned his head to point towards the sea.

"I will take care of this mess, sir," Rajan said, making sense of his boss's subtle command.

DK pulled out a cigar from his top pocket and put it in his mouth. Rajan gave him a light. "Find out where they have gone?" commanded DK.

"If they are smart, they will go to the police," Rajan said, "Or should I say fool?"

DK nodded. "Send our men. Dig the whole city. They can't go too far, their passports are with us."

"Yes, sir."

DK took a long drag from his cigar and moved in the direction of the sea. He stood at the veranda with wooden fences and looked at a distance into the vast Bay of Bengal. "One's decision can take one from bottom to the top or vice versa," he had always said. Though, he rarely felt proud of his own decisions. In his sixty years' life, he had regretted almost all his decisions. This was not any different. This whole week had been a week of horrible choices. First, he had placed his trust in some wrong people, which cost him a fortune. Two hundred million rubbles had been flushed through the gutter due to a leak in his circle. A large consignment of cocaine and arms that was supposed to be imported via sea and distributed in the country via various distributors was confiscated by the police.

This one, though, he knew would cost him more. He might have to pay with his life.

Leonid was the right hand of Vladimir, a Russian arms dealer, and mafia king. Nobody raised an eye on Leonid, let alone shoot him. But DK did. He had not only started gunfire with him but also managed to kill him in the process. He knew his own death was inevitable. His only hope was sealed inside that blood-red package, which refused to open.

He knew that nothing in this world would make Vladimir spare his life anymore, but that thing can at least make his death less painful. He knew, Vladimir never killed his victims once and for all. He would cause a man to die thousands of death before death actually came to him. Like a cat who would play with its prey for hours, teasing and torturing it until it gives up all hopes, becomes still and succumbs to pain.

He remembered the day when he first heard the name 'Vladimir'. It was the late 1970's. Daanish Khandiyar was a Doctoral student at Moscow State University. He had almost completed his Ph.D. in advanced cellular biology and needed only to submit his thesis before he could be granted the doctorate degree.

He was taking an afternoon nap in his hostel room. It was a typical twin-shared hostel room like any other in Russia or India – study table covered with numerous books of which few were never opened in months, chair converted into hangers used for drying clothes and underwear, walls decorated with poems, expletives, and graffiti, wooden cabinets with dangling doors, etc.

Without any warning, four Russian men barged into the room, breaking the weak wooden door into pieces. One of them pulled Daanish by his hair and dragged him off his bed. He pushed his head down hard as it banged against the floor. Daanish cried loud to be heard by the whole floor. The first man kicked hard on his face from left as it turned towards the right. He pressed his face with his shoe, letting his right cheek pressing against the cold floor. The three others joined him too and kicked the young DK repeatedly in his abdomen. Blood was oozing out of DK's mouth, and his shirt began to tear apart. He felt multiple ribs cracking inside his chest and his organs getting crushed by the percussions.

Two men came rushing into the room. One was a uniformed security guard who carried a thick wooden rod and other, warden of the hostel. They were reported by some students on the same floor of shouting. The guard dragged one of the men by his hand. The warden also pulled another man and yelled, "Stop it right now!"

Nobody listened and continued beating Daanish.

The security guard struck the man with his wooden baton. The man turned and snatched the rod from him with his strong muscular hands. He, then, started beating the guard with the rod and threw him on the floor and continued beating.

After a couple of minutes, they stopped beating DK and the guard and let go. They turned to leave. At the threshold, one of them turned and said, "Oh, I almost forgot, Max said 'hello' to you. Return his money in twenty-four hours, or he will have to come himself to catch a cup of coffee with you". He left.

DK tried to raise his head, but failed and spat out blood before falling into unconsciousness.

After many hours, DK found himself lying in a hospital bed. He turned his head left to see his friend-cum-roommate sitting by his side, who was gone since morning for some research work. He, too, was Indian and had directly rushed to the hospital upon receiving information about his best friend's exigency. He was tall, dark, and chew tobacco. He belonged to a royal family in Rajasthan, India. He had been in Russia for nine years when he got a scholarship for his post-graduation at the Moscow State University. His name was Sashikant.

"I had told you, you must give up gambling, or you will be into deep trouble one day," the young man said.

DK was having trouble opening his swollen mouth since his cheekbone was fractured from the assault. He somehow managed to articulate a few words, "Please help me."

"Of course, I will. What are friends for?" said the tobacco-chewing-man.

DK had been very serious for academics and had been an excellent student in his whole life. Until however, he made some bad acquaintances and got engaged in betting and gambling. Though he was never good at it. He made more losses than profit. Day by day, loss after loss, he exhausted almost all his savings. He started working as a waiter in a restaurant and spent all his earnings on gambling.

He used to do betting on horse races and international cricket too. One day, he was tipped by one of his acquaintances that a certain horse was surely going to win as the match was fixed. He was told that the betting rate on that horse was particularly low, and he had to place a large bet to make some significant profit. He was taken to Max, who was a local mafia who collected weekly money from the local vendors and threatened them to burn their shops if they didn't pay. He was also a contract killer and a local drug dealer.

DK approached Max for a loan and sanctioned himself five hundred thousand rubbles on a high-interest rate. He didn't worry about the interest because he knew he would return the money on the very next day after winning the bet.

Uneventfully, he won the bet but got robbed on his way by a thug. He lost all the money, including the principal and the profit made from the stake. He also lost his gold chain and watch. He was surely bankrupt. He was sure it was a planned robbery executed by Max's boys.

Max didn't come after him for eight months, but he did eventually and started threatening DK. At first, there were stalking, later there were abuses, threatening with weapons, slaps until this day when he was brutally assaulted. Max gave him a window of twenty-four hours to pay five hundred thousand rubbles, which was impossible for DK.

Sashikant, DK's friend, who had gone out of the hospital room, returned after some time. "I have solved your problem."

Young Daanish, unable to speak, gestured with his hand asking how.

"I called Vladimir to pay your debt. He is more powerful than Max and is happy to help," said Sashikant.

DK stared at his friend's face and waited for the word 'but'.

"But, you have to perform some easy tasks for him," Sashikant said, "Vladimir is a mafia king here as you may know. His control runs throughout Russia and even outside. He smuggles gold and other things in and out of the country. You will have to become a carrier. Since you are an Indian citizen, you will have to carry the things with you while you go meet your family in India, your travel expenses will be fully paid. Even I have also worked for him a couple of times for some extra money. Do this, and you will be free from all your debts."

Vladimir was indeed a king in the Russian mafia circles. His businesses included many illegitimate ones such as drug dealing, weapons dealing, contract killing, extortion, flesh trade, and smuggling among few legitimate ones such as import-export of toys, restaurant chains, and cab services. A major part of his black money came, indisputably, from smuggling. He would smuggle anything from girls to gold, diamond, and other taxable items. He would hire unsuspecting young people as his carriers. He transported gold and diamonds via these carriers as personal belongings passing through custom. His men followed various tricks to effortlessly pass these items through security checks, such as hiding them inside toys. They would follow some innovative tricks too, such as converting gold into gold dust and suspending it in water to decrease its density and pass through the x-ray. Some will insert well-packed diamonds, drugs, and precious stones in their rectums, which won't set off metal detectors. Though, these tricks had a failure rate of one in twenty. Yet Vladimir made a lot of money by this, and if somehow his trick failed, he would only lose one of his men and some number of smuggled items.

DK thought for a long time. He knew there were no other options except death. Max never thundered in vain. If he had said he would kill him in twenty-four hours, he would *indeed* kill him in twenty-four hours if he didn't pay his money back. Money didn't matter to these mafia men as much as the fear in the people for them did.

After futile attempts in search of a plausible way out of this menace, he finally agreed. He gave his friend a broken assenting nod.

"Are you sure?" Sashikant said, "You cannot refuse later."

DK nodded again.

"Okay, I'll tell him. He will settle your debts with Max. I'll fix a meeting for you when you are able to leave the bed." He put an assuring hand on DK's bandaged shoulder. "Everything will be fine," he assured.

A few weeks later, he met Vladimir personally and understood his task very carefully. That day was a turning point in his life – a major turnaround. He was expelled from the university by disciplinary action for the pandemonium caused in the hostel by him.

He worked for Vladimir for a long time. He travelled to India a dozen times in a year to smuggle goods, most of the time skipping a meet with his family to dodge suspecting eyes. He repaid his debts very soon. But his greed had taken good of him, and he started spending lavishly. Soon he became a prime apprentice to Vladimir.

One day Vladimir ordered him to permanently move to India and be his deputy there. DK agreed. He asked for some more money from Vladimir to set up a microbiology lab in Chennai. Since he had a post-graduate degree in Microbiology, it suited him best. Most of the research in his lab was conducted by hired scientists, and DK took the administrative role. Moreover, it allowed him to launder his money from other businesses.

DK came out of his reverie and watched Rajan dragging the motorboat out of the sea. He carried the dead bodies wrapped in plastic to the deep sea to dispose of. Rajan gave him a side-nod from the distance to say, "It's Done."

CHAPTER THIRTEEN

Samar eyed the tall metal gates at the entrance of the bungalow, where he and his friends were led to. It was a medium-sized two-storey beautiful house with a tiled roof. It had a small garden in front of it, but the plants were mostly dried up. The structure was old and seemed like not renovated in ages. It gave a feel of horror mixed with curiosity. Samar wondered who, if at all, lived in this place. He was about to find out.

The man from the car pushed open the metal door and waited for Zac, Piyu, Viren, and Samar to enter. They did reluctantly. They stood in front of an old red-brown coloured double door made with polished teakwood. The nameplate over it stated, "Dr. Adhusudhan Mukherjee, Psychologist." The old man rang the doorbell. It took a couple of minutes before they heard somebody unbolting the opaque wooden door.

A woman opened the door partly and stood at the threshold. She was old, just like the man who had ferried them to that place. She wore a light green saree and a couple of bangles that jingled as she adjusted her bifocal eye-glasses. She scanned her guests one-by-one carefully. Then she looked at the old man and smiled. "You didn't tell me there are going to be guests today," she said.

Samar and his friends were offered seats on an old but sturdy sofa set. The old lady came through the kitchen with a tray holding four glasses of Roohafza and placed on the low-hung table wooden table.

The old man sat on a high backed sofa chair, facing his young guests, his hostages to be more precise. "Take a gulp," he ordered.

Samar scowled at the old man defiantly. The old man stared back at him. His stern, penetrating gaze never left Samar for once. "Have it, you must be thirsty," he said.

Samar looked at the glasses and then at the woman. He picked one of the glasses and pushed the dark red sweet liquid down his throat. His friends followed.

"You want more?" asked the old woman.

The old man waited until the woman collected all the glasses and disappeared into the kitchen. He said in a deep but fading Bengali-accented voice, "I liked your previous name more."

"Who are you?" Samar demanded.

"Of course, how could you remember me? You were just five," the man said more to himself than others.

Samar watched silently.

The man took a minute before replying, "My name is Adhusudhan Mukherjee. Your father and I were friends."

"Really? You make a hell of a friend, then. Kidnapping your friend's son seems not much friendly to me."

The old man ignored his comment and continued, "You used to visit my place. You used to call me Sudhan uncle. Your father and I used to take you fishing to the open sea in my boat. Your name was Naman, back then."

Samar frowned. Nobody except his uncle knew about his other name. His uncle never mentioned it to anyone, and neither did he. His new identity kept him safe from the mischievous DK for twenty years. And yet this man, who claims to be a friend of his father, seemed to know about it. Was the man really who he said to be.

"Even if I believe, just for a minute," Samar started, "that you and my father were friends and you knew me personally. Still, what do you want from us now? Is it only me who thinks that we all are taken hostages here." He looked at his friends.

"I was asked by my friend, your father Jaswant, to keep an eye on you. When I learnt that you were returning to India, more importantly, Chennai, I was doing just so – keeping an eye on you."

"What with the gun thing, then?" Samar asked.

"You were right. I was bluffing. If I had tried to explain it to you there, you would never understand. That's why I had to take drastic steps."

"We were going to the police."

"That would have been of no use. The legal process of this country is as rusty as it gets. You would have only disclosed your location to DK, and then we all know what he could do."

Samar intently watched every expression on the old man's face and finally sighed. "What do you know about my father?" he inquired.

"Everything."

"Were you close friends?"

"Very close. We were childhood friends. What do you youngsters call it, aah, *chuddie-buddies*," the old man sighed. "Even our *fathers* were very close friends. We shared the same neighbourhood."

The old woman returned with a little girl. In her pre-teen, she was a charming little girl. Her dark waist-long black hair was tied with a yellow hair-band and had subtle curls at the end. Her facial features were cutely curvy and would, indubitably, attract a second look. She wore a blue-white knee-length frock and a stud 'bindi' on her forehead.

Mukherjee turned to welcome them. "This is my wife, you've already met. With her is our sole cause of living, the apple of our eyes, our granddaughter – Muskaan."

Samar waved his hand, always in lack of words with kids. Piyu smiled and raised her hand, flapping her fingers up and down as a hello.

"She lost her parents when she was two," Mukherjee uttered in a saddened voice.

Piyu's eyes were widened in horror. There was no pity in her eyes, but a lot of affection for the poor child.

Viren passed a sympathetic smile to the little girl. "What happened?"

"The tsunami. The sea soared and claimed thousands of lives. 26th December 2004," Mukherjee paused. "It was her birthday. They were coming from a late-night dinner when the huge wave touched the shore." He took off his eyeglasses to wipe the drop of tear that welled up in his eyes. He wore the glasses back and continued, "had we been with them too, she would have become a total orphan. God knows what would have happened to this beautiful soul then."

There was dead silence in the room.

"She was missing for three months before we reached the orphanage in search of her and found her there. She was saved by some locals and taken over to the police. But she had no identity on her and was too young to give them an address or number. We had been searching everywhere, people had told us to give up hope, but we didn't."

"She's a lovely child. You must be proud of her," Samar said, eyeing the girl, who hid behind the old lady.

"We indeed are. She is so calm and content. We never had any trouble raising her without her parents. But I wonder what will happen to her if we don't live long enough to find a loving husband for her. That's why we want her to become independent, to live her life with dignity and pride. May God bless her!"

"God bless," Piyu wished.

Mukherjee took a deep sigh. He looked at Samar and asked, "tell me one thing how did you manage to evade DK?"

"To spare the gory details, he was engaged in a shootout, which bought us enough time to escape."

"You're lucky enough, at least luckier than your father."

"My father? Did *DK* kill my father?" there was a sudden flood of anger and impatience in Samar's voice.

"I am not sure. But he was in a run from DK. He had come to meet me a few days before his accident. He was in a hurry. About five days later, his car fell into the Coovum River just before the mouth of the Napier's bridge. Police couldn't find his car for weeks as the river drained into the sea less than a mile away. His decomposed body was found buckled to the driver seat of his car a month later and was identified from his belongings. Your father was a good swimmer; perhaps he couldn't unbuckle himself in time."

"What about my mother?"

"Your mother was nowhere to be found after the accident. Few witnesses confirmed her leaving from their house with your father right before the accident. They couldn't find her, neither dead nor alive. She was assumed dead after a few months."

"There was some Prof. Gowda, whose research my father had been hiding from DK this whole time. What happened to him? How did *he* die?" Samar spoke inquisitively.

"He committed suicide in his own office. It was there in the newspapers the next day."

"Is there any chance DK was behind his death?" Samar said. Piyu, Zac, and Viren listened carefully.

"He might be the reason, but he was not the killer. Guru was protecting his research. He knew if he got captured by DK, everything would be tortured out of him, and he couldn't afford that. But DK didn't kill him. It was undoubted."

"Why would you say that?"

"Because Guru was his childhood friend. In fact, I, your father, Guru, and DK were all childhood friends. We lived in the same railway colony. My father was the section officer, your grandfather was station master, Guru's father was a TT, and DK's father was store in-charge. Despite our different backgrounds, we were best friends. We were raised together by our parents. Later in our lives, our paths diverged as we changed countries to further our education. Guru remained here and studied at IIT Madras. After graduation, I moved to London to study psychology. Your father graduated in Chemical Engineering here and got a scholarship at the University of Southern California. DK too graduated from IIT-M, but later joined Moscow State University for Master's on a scholarship."

"But DK did not seem like someone with a good education, did he?" Zac said.

"He was at some time. It was when he got addicted to gambling that he lost his sanity and turned evil. He had lost a lot of money and joined Vladimir, a Russian mafia god, in various illicit jobs. He started weapons and drug trafficking in and out of India on behalf of Vladimir. His Delta Research Lab is just a cover-up for his illegal businesses."

"How come DK didn't come after you?" Samar enquired.

"'cause he never knew I was in India, let alone in touch with Guru. After finishing my studies, I stayed back in London and practised psychology. Later, when I shifted back to India, I contacted Guru. He told me about DK and his recent despicable activities. He told me to stay away from him as he was no more the same DK as he used to be. Later, I met your father too. We stayed in contact until one day…"

There was silence.

"I do not understand," Piyu said, wondering, "Prof. Gowda wanted to sell the HIV vaccine on his own and didn't want to give any credit to DRL. His sole aim was money. But he preferred to kill himself before letting DK name his invention. What would he do with all that money if he was dead?"

"That's an intelligent question. But it seems like you have some incomplete information." There was a halo of mystery behind the old man's voice. "But I think you should take some rest first. You all look tired. There are a couple of bedrooms vacant in this house. Go be fresh and try to get some sleep. You are safe here."

The quartet agreed readily as they were in desperate need of sound sleep for their brains to work properly. Their bodies were working overtime in this whole turmoil.

They were offered some sambhar rice – one of the south-Indian delicacies. After that, they retired to the three vacant rooms. Viren and Piyu took the two guestrooms on the upper storey. Zac and Samar shared one bedroom on the ground floor. They all took a thorough bath and then sank into their beds to get some afternoon sleep.

Later that day, after a few hours' sleep, Zac and Samar moved out of their bedroom. It was post-evening and night had fallen. They found Mr. Mukherjee's wife and his granddaughter occupied the sofa. The old lady was telling stories to the girl as she caressed her head. The girl leaned into her grandmother's bosom. She sat straight up, seeing the men walking her way.

"Hi, Musky! Good Evening to you," Zac spoke endearingly as they sat on the opposite sofa.

"Hi," she replied.

"Beta! Do you want some coffee or tea?" the old lady offered.

"Yes, Mrs. Mukherjee. But please let me make it," Zac replied.

"No, no. Don't take me for old. It's just the wrinkles. I am still as strong as ever," Mrs. Mukherjee said.

"No, I didn't mean like that. I really liked your sambhar. I thought I will make you try our Australian-style coffee. Our Musky can show me the kitchen, won't you, dear?"

"Of course. Muskaan! Will you help *bhaiyya*?"

Muskaan nodded.

Zac stood up and extended a hand towards the little girl. She took his hand and led him to the kitchen.

A few minutes later, Mr. Mukherjee emerged out of the bathroom. He smiled, looking at Samar.

"Good evening, Sudhan uncle," Samar said.

"Good evening, my son," Mr. Mukherjee replied enthusiastically. "Had a sound sleep?"

Later, Viren also climbed down the stairs and joined the men. Zac came out of the kitchen with a tray holding six mugs of coffee. Muskaan followed with a plate of biscuits. He placed a mug of coffee in front of each of them. "Come on, Musky, we will go upstairs to give Piyu a cup of coffee too," Zac said, holding the tray with two mugs in one hand and Muskaan's hand in his other.

Zac knocked on the door. Piyu took a minute to open the door. "Hello, Piyu! Muskaan and I have made some coffee for you."

"Aw, how sweet of you!" Piyu bent down to give a peck on Muskaan's cheek. "Come on in. I was standing on the balcony. It's such a lovely weather outside."

Zac and Piyu stood in the balcony holding a mug of coffee each. Muskaan stood beside them. The weather was indeed lovely. With the onset of monsoon, the climate in Chennai turned heavenly. A slow scented breeze blew and played with the tall coconut trees. Though, there was no view from the balcony since it was shadowed by two very tall coconut trees. The breeze was extremely pleasant. The moment was so romantic one could fall in love with anyone, and that is what was happening to Zac. He was falling in love with Piyu, again and again, each day more passionately.

"So, Musky! Which grade are you in?" Piyu asked softly.

"I am in fifth standard," Muskaan replied in a cute voice.

"Oh, wow! You are a big girl now," Piyu replied. "I love your dress. Would you like to go shopping with me someday? I could really use your help in finding such a beautiful dress for me too."

Muskaan gave a childish sideward nod.

"Amazing! Thank you so much," Piyu said.

"Can I go downstairs? Grandma said she will help me with my homework. She sleeps early," said Muskaan coyly.

"Sure, baby. Do you want me to help you with your homework?" asked Piyu.

"No. Thank you. My grandma always helps me with my homework," Muskaan replied.

"Okay, you go then. Good night. Love you," Piyu gave her a flying kiss.

Muskaan blushed and ran away.

"She's such a lovely girl. God always has to play dirty tricks with lovely people," Piyu said to Zac.

Downstairs, Mr. Mukherjee told Samar many things about Jaswant. He told him about his indigenous research projects for the military. He also told him about Jaswant's unusual behaviour one week before his demise. Samar and Viren listened to the stories for one hour. "Would you like to have a drink?" Mr. Mukherjee offered.

"No, sir. Thank You. I would go upstairs now," Viren said and stood up to leave.

"I'll have a drink," Samar replied.

"Scotch?"

"Yeah."

Mr. Mukherjee pulled out a bottle of Millburn Single Malt Scotch whisky and poured some of it in two glasses with two cubes of ice in each. He moved towards the front door and gestured Samar to follow.

Samar rose from his seat and followed the old man to the lawn. He took one of the glasses from Mr. Mukherjee. They stood under a coconut tree and enjoyed their drinks with the cool evening breeze.

"Sudhan, uncle!" called Samar softly.

"Yes, my son?"

"The question Piyu had asked in the afternoon."

"That, why did Gurudutt Gowda commit suicide?"

"Yes. We've been told that he had discovered a vaccine for HIV, and he wanted to earn lots of unshared money. But at last, he forced himself to take his life. Why would someone do that?"

"That's because you have been misinformed," Mukherjee said. "It's true that Guru was working on a vaccine for HIV for over a decade. But that thing sealed in that package is not a vaccine but the disease itself."

"Yes, I know that Prof. Gowda used genetically modified HIV to protect against HIV. But what's in that?"

"No. You don't understand. Prof. Gowda *tried* to use modified HIV to protect against HIV. But what he had discovered was nothing as he had planned."

"What was that, then?"

"Guru wanted to test the vaccine by administering it into apes. He experimentally infected few simians with a modified virus by using an SIV-HIV hybrid that every other researcher does to conduct pre-clinical testing of a potential HIV vaccine. He monitored the apes, and it showed some promising results as the disease had not progressed for many days. He watched the apes showing constant viral load for several days. But, one day suddenly, the apes' condition degraded rapidly. He tried everything to save them, but he could only give them a day more. But what happened after that was frightening, to say the least. The apes not only died but decayed unrecognizably."

"Oh my god! It means the vaccine was never successful," exclaimed Samar.

"No. I have seen the Polaroid photo of the dead animals. They seemed like they had died and been rotten for several weeks. But Guru said they died only fifteen hours before taking the photo. He suspected that the modified virus had somehow mutated and been able to infect every cell of the body rather than only immune cells. It triggered necrosis – uncontrolled death of living cells and tissues – as in gangrene. It was a frightful scene to look at. Guru intended to run a probe on the cause of the mutation to see if it was just random or there was a certain cause for the mutation. He didn't live long enough to tell us what he found out."

"Wait a minute. It means DK knew there was no vaccine. Then why is he still after that thing even after such a long time. What will he do with a failed…," Samar paused as he realized the other alternative, the horrible, horrendous alternative. "He wants to use it as a weapon – a biological weapon. Doesn't he?"

"Yes. You're just as intelligent as your father. He works for Vladimir, who supplies weapons into the black market. Many people would be interested in this type of weapon – terrorist groups, governments."

"A virus that kills in days, not weeks, will give no time to develop a cure. It will wreak havoc on earth. Whoever holds it will dominate the whole world."

"To worsen the case, the virus had gone airborne. Since it could infect any cell, it didn't require sexual contact or blood transfusion to communicate. It could invade an organism through the lungs too. They had to incinerate a whole section of the lab and were just lucky that they didn't catch the virus themselves. Guru said if this kind of virus was left unmonitored and allowed to communicate rapidly. It will take only a week to completely destroy the ecosystem. There will be only carcasses – decayed, rotten carcasses of humans and animals everywhere."

"But why anyone would let this monster out when it meant near extinction of the humans. Whom will he rule, if everyone is dead?"

"One does not need to launch this kind of weapon. Mere possession of this thing will give him the ultimate power. There will be a shift of world powers. He could invade any country, and no one could stop him. Governments will be forced to form alliance with him, and he will be paid with a huge amount of money to keep this monster chained."

"We need to destroy that thing immediately," Samar said with a hint of desperation.

"Yes, we do. But DK has become a wild dog now. It will take more than a moonlight requisition to get the research out of his claws. However, if we destroy the solution to open that package, the sealed package will not be of any use to anyone."

It suddenly started raining heavily. Both of them were forced to run back into the house quickly.

Mrs. Mukherjee shouted from inside, "come in fast. Dinner is ready."

Samar followed the old psychologist inside and closed the wooden door behind them.

One storey above, Zac and Piyu stood together on the balcony. They watched the men having a serious discussion. Though, their speech was incomprehensible from this distance. Yet, it took no effort to understand from their expressions that they were not discussing the weather. It must be related to their current predicament.

The sudden onset of rainfall forced Piyu and Zac to rush inside.

"That was untold of," Piyu said.

"You don't like rains?" Zac enquired.

"Are you kidding? I love rain," Piyu replied, putting their mugs on the bedside table. "Isn't it so romantic?"

"It is. I too love rain. When we were kids, Samar and I would dance in the rain every time. Rain means fun to me."

"For me, it means love and romance. But sadly, I recently broke up from a serious relationship." Piyu pouted.

"Yeah, I heard you speaking to that boy in the mall. You must be upset right now?"

"Nah! I never loved him, actually. He was too possessive, and I was always doubtful of the relationship. And, his final words have made it easier for me to forget him," said Piyu. "You tell me how many girlfriends you had?" she enquired

"None."

"None?! Are you kidding? You seem like a person to me who would have half a dozen girlfriends at a single time," Piyu nudged in his belly playfully.

"On the contrary, I have had only one girlfriend. That too was a teenage fling and didn't complete even three months," the brown-haired Australian shrugged.

"Really? It means you're still a…?" Piyu let Zac complete the sentence.

"Umm…Virgin? Yes," he said sheepishly.

"Well…that certainly came as a shock," Piyu said, extending her hand to catch falling raindrops. "Hey! You know what. Let's go in the rain."

"No. Come on, we don't have any spare clothes," Zac said little too late as he was dragged quickly by Piyu out onto the balcony.

Piyu turned back towards Zac and climbed over the concrete railing taking her forearms as leverage. She held Zac's hands in her own.

Zac looked directly into Piyu's eyes, having a hard time keeping himself from kissing her.

Unknown to Zac and anyone else, Piyu too once had a crush on him. She still remembered the day eight years ago at Sam's house party when she had noticed him for the first time. He wore a tuxedo, gifted to him by Samar's uncle. She was standing alone. He was talking to some boys. A few minutes later, the boys left him and went on to some other place. He turned to her direction. Piyu watched his dark brown hair jumping up and down as he walked towards her. His cute sparkling smile gave her a skip of a beat. Zac had been having some facial hair and had trimmed for the first time for the party. She looked at his black bow tie perfectly wrapped around his neck. He was closing in. There he was only a few feet away from her. She wanted him to look at her and talk to her. He came closer, and then suddenly, their eyes met. She was sure he noticed her. How couldn't he? She was wearing a sky-blue noodle strap dress, which ended well above her knee. She had recently started using make-up and had used a blue eye shadow and mascara. But sadly to her, he walked past her in a swift. She was sure he had noticed her. That was the starting of a three-year-old crush. It was the longest she liked someone. Slowly, gradually it faded out into anonymity. But she always wanted him to approach her and make friends with her. She was oblivious to the fact that Zac also wanted the same thing from himself.

"Piyu didi, Zac bhaiya," Muskaan rushed in, saying. "Please come downstairs, grandma is calling you for dinner," she spoke and left as swiftly as she came.

"Come on, let's go," Zac said.

"Yeah," Piyu said and raised herself on her forearms to climb down the railing. Suddenly, her hands slipped over the wet railing, and she fell backwards.

Zac caught Piyu by her bare legs just in time. Her legs were wet and slippery, and most of her weight had fallen beyond the point of support. It was increasingly difficult for Zac to keep her holding in place. He put his weight on her legs and lunged forward to catch her hands. "Come on, Piyu, give me your hand," he yelled.

Piyu crunched her abdomen and stretched her arm towards Zac. In two attempts, he finally caught her hand and started pulling her up. With his muscular arms, it took no more than a few seconds for him to pull her up completely. On reaching over the railing, she clutched him in her arms tightly. She gave him a kiss on his neck. "Thank you. Thank you so much, Zac. I love you," she said. She hugged him for some more time.

Viren watched the scene playing on the balcony from inside Piyu's room. He turned back quietly and left.

CHAPTER FOURTEEN

The next day, Mr. Mukherjee took his visitors to his study. He pulled out a small metal box from his huge cabinet, hosting a large number of books on Psychology and other subjects. The old man put it down gently over the study desk without making any noise. It was a heavy grey metal locker box 15"x12"x12" in dimensions. The front surface was slightly indented inwards but had no handle to pull it open.

Samar and his friends leaned in to take a closer look. *Another sealed box* they wondered.

"What's this?" Samar enquired.

"This is what your father bequeathed to me on his last day. He asked me to keep it protected until someone comes in search of it," Mr. Mukherjee informed.

"This seems like some locker. What's inside it?" asked Viren.

"Probably, the solution to open this seal," Piyu suggested pointing to the blue package in Samar's hand.

"Might be. I am not sure. I have never taken a look inside it," said the old man, who put a hand on the box.

"But how do we open it?" Zac said, "There's no handle or keyhole."

"There's one keyhole on the left face," Mukherjee said, turning the box clockwise for everyone to see. It was a small hole about one-inch in diameter. It was neither circular nor the standard circle-over-a-rectangle keyhole shape. It was irregular, somewhat resembling the Greek letter 'delta' – δ.

"This doesn't look like a keyhole. This is so absurd," Piyu said, moving her finger in and about the hole.

"It indeed is," Samar said, "And we have the key."

Everyone grasped instantly what he meant. Samar took out the quasi-cylindrical metal object from his pants' pocket. He tried to insert it into the hole. It was slightly larger and wouldn't go in. He flipped it to insert it by the other end. It was the same at both ends and didn't go by either.

"We need a code to make it work," he declared.

"Do you have that code?" Zac asked.

"I think I do," he replied.

"Really?" Piyu asked excitedly.

"I had been thinking about this thing in an attempt to find the code since yesterday morning," Samar started to explain. "Suddenly, while sleep didn't come to me last night, something came up in my mind. I was recollecting memories of my childhood when it brought back to me how my uncle gifted a sort of piggy bank to me on one New Year's morning. I was probably six at that time. He wanted to teach me to save money on my own. That, the piggy bank had dialler combination lock with precisely seven digits sequence. I had broken that thing one day some six years later. My uncle brought me a similar piggy bank, and interestingly, it had the same lock code. He had customized the lock. I asked him why he chose the same number as it was too long and difficult to remember. He told me that it was an important number, and I should remember it until I die. He said it was my father's favourite number," Samar cherished the memories of his uncle who was no more standing by his side as always to hold him whenever he needed support. "I was too young to question that time. I preserved that thing for another four to five years. I was not a good saver. I finally lost it somewhere around my house and forgot to tell my uncle. He too never remembered to ask."

"Oh your piggy bank," Zac said, "I too remember it. It was a pink swine and had a small door in its butt where you rotate the dials to enter the code, and it opens to show the empty belly of the piggy. You, indeed, were not a good saver. You called it 'hoggie', didn't you? You still remember the code?"

"That's the issue. I don't. I didn't follow my uncle's command. We were growing into adults. Our brains were developing so many new memories; they just shaded this little number, which I didn't care enough for anyway. Hey Zac! I shared everything with you. I may have told you the number."

"Yes, you did," Zac said, "You told me I could use your piggy bank anytime I wish. But I never used it. I didn't remember the code for much longer."

"I can recall its first three digits; they were 7, 2, and 3."

"I remember there was a 4 and a 5. But I don't remember the sequence," Zac said apologetically.

"We have come to a dead-end, then," Samar said despondently.

"It means we can't open this thing?" Piyu asked.

"Why don't you break it open?" suggested Viren.

"I don't want this thing to open. I want to destroy the solution," said Samar.

"Why? What about the research?" asked Piyu.

"Why don't we just hand it over to DK. His methods may be wrong and a little selfish. But ultimately, it will help society. Many people can be saved by the vaccine. Why destroy it?"

"Actually," Samar said and paused to look at Mukherjee, who gave him a nod to go on. "That thing, in that red package, is not a vaccine. It's a deadly virus, a potential biological weapon," he added.

"What?" everyone uttered in unison.

"Yes. The research never succeeded. The recombinant virus Prof Gowda designed mutated in a deadlier virus than HIV. It was as incurable as HIV, plus it took only days, not years to kill the victim. It's the Lord of Death himself waiting to be unleashed. If let out, it won't save millions but rather kill them, practically in an instant. It leaves the victim dead and rotten from within and moves on to its next prey by any means."

"MY GOD!!!" Viren uttered, placing a hand on top of his head.

"DK wants it to use it as a weapon, doesn't he?" Zac said inquisitively.

"DRL is just a cover-up. He's a drugs and weapons dealer in the country. And Vladimir, he mentioned once, is a Russian mafia leader," revealed Samar to his friends. He watched their eyes widened in horror upon receiving the mind-boggling information.

"Then why do you want to open this box? Just throw it into the sea and be relaxed about it," said the Australian young man.

"I wanted to make sure if it really contains the solution. Maybe it is just another clue. We could have thrown it into the sea and later realized that the solution is still lying unscathed at some other location. DK, with so many resources, can easily bypass this clue and follow the next. It's just a matter of time."

"Let's break it open then," Viren suggested.

"No. What if it contained another sealed package and it gets burnt by the impact," Piyu exhorted. "We should follow all the leads to the solution itself and then wreck it."

"I thought that too," Samar stared at the box.

"Then we're back to square one. We can neither unlock it nor break it open," Zac gave words to what everyone felt in that room, "We're stuck."

"There's another way," Mukherjee said, who had been standing speechlessly till that time. His audience looked at him mystified, wondering what way could follow the dead end.

"You said you remember the code for a long time but do not recall it now. It means it still lies somewhere inside your memory," Mukherjee smiled.

Everyone waited for the old man to make his point.

"I will suggest you try hypnotism," he finally said.

"Hypnotism?" Samar questioned.

"Yes. It can make you recall the information that is hidden deep inside your memory."

"Sudhan uncle," Samar replied dolefully, "I don't think I truly believe in these things?"

"These things? You're not confusing hypnotism with sorcery or black magic, are you son?" Mr. Mukherjee said, surprised.

Samar drew a blank face. His friends, too, remained sceptical.

"Hypnosis *actually* works. Humans have been using this technique since ancient times. There are numerous instances of people using hypnosis for various good and evil purposes in ancient Egypt and India. Gypsies, nowadays, use this technique on unsuspecting people to rob them of their belongings without even letting them realize that they're being robbed. Even a few animals create hypnosis, such as a cuttlefish, which mesmerizes its prey by changing its colour rapidly in weird fashion until it moves dangerously close to it for a successful attack."

Piyu looked at Zac, who shrugged.

"Haven't you heard the tale about the man who had lost his eyesight in a mustard gas attack during World War I? He was taken to a remarkable psychiatrist of that time – Edmund Forster. Forster hypnotized him and sent him in a state of complete trance. Once he was in a mentally vulnerable stage, the psychiatrist whispered something in his ear. He told him that he was no ordinary man. He was born special. Anyone with his divine powers could easily overcome the blindness and also rule the world. The man recovered his eyesight immediately after the session and also went on to almost rule the world. His name was Adolph Hitler. People say that he also developed some hypnotic powers of his own that made him an excellent orator as he was able to hypnotize his audience every time he gave a speech."

The quartet awed in wonder.

"Are you sure it will help in my case, too, Sudhan uncle?" Samar interrogated.

"Yes. One hundred percent," the old man replied.

"You too are a psychiatrist, aren't you?" Piyu said, "I saw the nameplate."

"I was. Now I am old and retired," Mr. Mukherjee said, "Moreover, I was never a specialist in hypnotherapy. Though, I know someone who can help you. He's been an intern under my mentorship when he started practicing psychiatry. Now he is a renowned psychiatrist and therapist. I will give him a call and fix you an urgent appointment."

Samar nodded in acceptance.

CHAPTER FIFTEEN

Samar sat at the clinic of the psychiatrist-cum-hypnotherapist recommended by Mr. Mukherjee. Only one of his friends was allowed to accompany him in the therapy chamber, rest were asked to wait outside. Samar chose Zac to follow as he shared his childhood with him. He could testify the descriptions, which Samar would give in his hypnotic state, to be accurate and not so-called 'pseudo-memories' that are often associated with hypnosis.

Samar was offered to drink a special honey-infused herbal tea to calm his nerves before the session began. He half-lied on a black leather-covered recliner. An electric atomizer sprayed a natural garden-like fragrance into the air. A slow, repetitive sound of splashing and trickling water played at the back with gradually decreasing tempo.

"Are you sure, Doctor, that it can help me recall a whole seven-digit number that I forgot a very long time ago?" Samar questioned.

"There's no hundred percent guarantee. But you still have some reasonable chances. In hypnosis, people develop a condition called *hypermnesia*, in which they can give a detailed account of long-forgotten events. It is more difficult for old people because many of their nerve cells are damaged due to aging. But with someone of your age, it is pretty straightforward. And as I have been informed, the information stayed with you for a long span of time, I am sure you should be able to recall it without any effort."

Samar was asked to watch the projector screen that hung straight before him at some distance. Initially, the projector showed some bright coloured circles that changed patterns first rapidly, then slowly to tire the subject's eyes. Later, the projector showed five black-and-white spiralling circles called *hypnodisks* – the biggest one at the centre surrounded by four small ones at the corners. Samar focused his attention on the screen. The first four initial attempts were futile as Samar couldn't retain a state of trance for a long time. He awoke whenever he was asked to describe his childhood. In the fifth attempt, however, he was thrown into a deep hypnotic state. The therapist, this time, started with asking something about more recent topics such as his current business endeavours, his last vacation spot, et cetera. Gradually, he took Samar deeper into his childhood. He was asked to describe his high-school friends and his teachers.

After dwelling for a long time in Samar's childhood, the therapist asked him to remember the special code that had been part of his memory for quite a long time. It took little persuasion and patience in the therapist's part. Samar finally recalled the number. Zac was also able to recall the number as soon as Samar uttered the sequence. He testified it.

The therapist wrote down the sequence on a paper and gave it to Zac. He, then, brought Samar out from his hypnotic state of mind. He remembered everything that had happened during the session.

He removed the weird key from his pocket and started rotating the dials. He entered the seven digits numeric code and waited. Nothing happened. He pressed the top of the key, and it suddenly clicked. A familiar delta-δ shaped protrusion came out of the bottom of the key.

"That's it," Zac uttered.

Samar, accompanied by Zac, Piyu, and Viren, reached Mr. Mukherjee's bungalow only to find a massive commotion in front of it.

There was a crowd collected near the house. They heard police sirens blaring outside the gate.

When Samar and his friends rushed into the bungalow, they were stopped by two policemen.

Samar tried to push his way in. "What happened here? We were here a few hours ago. Let us go in," he cried.

The quartet was allowed to go in. They found several police officers wandering inside the house, frantically searching the whole premises. Samar rushed towards the farthest corner of the house, only to find many policemen standing in a circle. As they reached closer, they finally saw it. Two dead bodies lay covered in blank white sheets. Muskaan sat in the corner held by a lady officer.

Samar and his friends took no moment to realize that the elderly couple they saw only a few hours ago has departed from this world. There was no doubt that it was DK who somehow had located them. Samar instantly felt guilty and blamed himself for bringing death to the old man's doorsteps.

Piyu felt extremely sorry for the poor kid who had already lost her parents and now her grandparents. She circled around the group of uniform-clad men and reached Muskaan. She bent down and pulled Muskaan in her arms. Muskaan turned around and hugged the beautiful young woman whom she had started to like since last night. Piyu hugged the little girl tightly and stroked her back. Muskaan cried loudly and wrapped her arms around Piyu's neck.

Viren talked to a constable who stood bolted at some distance from the crime spot. He asked him about what had happened at the place.

"Murder," said the policeman and added, "Two close-range bullet shots in the chest, when the wife came back after buying groceries. She was shot in the head from six feet distance. Her body was found at the door. The kid somehow hid herself under the kitchen slab."

Samar kneeled beside the still body of the man whom he had, lately, started regarding next to his deceased father. He uncovered the face from under the white sheet. Samar remembered the old man as he saw him just a few hours ago – joyful, lively, and full of energy. Although the face of the sexagenarian was covered with vague wrinkles, yet he looked far under his age as if he defied aging.

Now, however, the face of the man who was lying on the floor covered in blank white sheets looked different. The dark complexion of the man had turned darker. His right cheek and his salt-pepper beard were stained with clotted blood. His expression, however, was frozen in peacefulness. It was no doubt that the old man had seen his impending death as the killer had shot him from the front. It appeared, though, as the old man wasn't in denial and accepted his fate whole-heartedly. Samar looked at the blood-smeared face of the dead man, which had turned into a grotesque. It acted as a *Memento Mori* for him – reminding him that one has to die, be whatever.

Samar rose and looked at Viren and Zac. "How on earth he found us – that stinking son of a bitch?" he asked.

Zac dashed to the study. He looked at the table and found the locker missing from where he had seen it the last time. He looked everywhere between the shelves but didn't find it. He searched carefully through the books and surprisingly found the blue package lying indistinctly between them. He was sure that Mr. Mukherjee must have managed to hide it there before he got killed.

He ran to his friends and furnished the ill-news. He showed them the blue package and told them that the locker was nowhere to be seen.

The constable who talked to Samar earlier moved closer to them upon seeing the package, which appeared as some potential evidence. He held Zac by his arm and asked, "What is this thing?"

"Listen!" Samar said to the junior policeman. "We have some information about this mishap and about many other things. We want to talk to your investigating in-charge, right now."

"Okay! Come with me," the constable started walking towards the main door. He moved out of the house with Samar, Zac, and Viren in tow. Piyu had also joined them, leaving Muskaan in her bed.

The quartet followed the policeman to a police car. They saw a senior official standing by the car, discreetly speaking into a cellphone. They approached him and stopped at some distance.

The senior policeman gave a thorough searching look to the young fellows as he continued talking on his phone. He was a middle-aged man. He wore the usual khaki police uniform with a cap. Three golden stars adorned each of the shoulders of his half-sleeve khaki shirt. The black badge on his left shirt pocket stated, 'ACP Rakesh Makhija'. He was tall, little too dark, and fashioned a trimmed moustache. His usual service gun – .32 colt pistol – was covered in the bolster that hung by his brown uniform belt.

The policeman took more than a couple of minutes to finish his call. He finally ended his call and put the cell phone inside his pant pocket. He turned to the constable who recently approached him and asked, "Have forensics reached yet?"

"No, sir. On their way," the junior replied.

"Consistent," uttered the ACP. "Who are they?" he asked, addressing Samar and his companions. He looked at the four youngsters one by one. He took more time looking at the small package in Samar's hands.

"Sir, they wanted to meet you. They have some information about this case," said the constable.

"Who are you people?" the ACP asked, "What is the thing in your hands?"

"Sir, My name is Samar Oza. I am an Australian resident of Indian origin. These are my friends," Samar explained everything that had happened in the last half-week. He told the police official about DK, about Gowda and his research, his father and his role in the whole scenario, and finally, Mr. Mukherjee, who lost his life recently amidst this pandemonium.

The Assistant Commissioner of Police listened intently to everything the young man and his friend had to offer.

Samar also explained the significance of the metal box currently in their possession. He told him about the grave consequences that could befall if DK had to get his hands on whatever lay inside the box.

The ACP was shocked by the stunningly dangerous information that passed through his ears. He stood silent for a long time, watching the people in front of him and contemplating his next move. After scrutinizing the situation for some time, he finally said, "this thing is really big. We have been following DK for many months now. Recently, we have apprehended few boys with a very large consignment of smuggled items in their possession. We have insider input that DK is involved in the smuggling of those items. Since then, our team has been keeping close eyes on the man. You're the first of the eyewitness of any sort that we have acquired. Your revelation can be a breakthrough in the investigation."

"Sir, we believe DK is a very dangerous man, and you need to arrest him as quickly as possible. We know where he lives," Viren spoke.

"That we too know," the ACP said, "But we can't arrest anyone just like that. We need some shreds of evidence before we get an arrest warrant. You guys have to come with me."

"Where?" asked Samar.

"This thing is big. I will have to consult my senior officers before I can take any steps. We should go to the headquarters. You will have to tell them what you have just told me."

"Fine," said Samar. He looked at his friends, who nodded in acceptance.

Samar and his friends were asked to enter the ACP's service vehicle – a seven-seater Black Mahindra Scorpio with a blue beacon light on top. A large circular logo of the Chennai Metropolitan Police was printed on the bonnet of the SUV, below which printed was the motto of the Chennai Police – Truth Alone Triumphs, above it, was the Tamil translation of the same.

They were accompanied by the ACP Makhija himself and his subordinates – two of his constables on duty. One of the constables buckled his seatbelt, ready to start the engine, while the ACP took the front passenger seat. Viren sat between Zac and the other constable in the middle row. Samar climbed through the rear gate and took one of the side-facing seats. He helped Piyu climb into the vehicle and sit on the seat facing his own.

The driver ignited the engine and pulled the police vehicle swiftly through the comparably thinner afternoon traffic of Chennai roads.

Samar was mostly lost in thoughts of today's events, occasionally chatting with the senior police officer getting more information about DK and his illicit businesses. At many times, Samar felt as if the ACP talked about the evil smuggler-cum-murderer   more   admiringly   than contemptuously. He told him about how DK's criminal circle included most of the prominent drug dealers and weapons supplier in the city, yet how he managed to evade traps laid by police several times.

Zac and Viren sat quietly, listening to the exchange of information between their friend and the officer.

Piyu, however, looked outside and missed most of the conversation happening inside the vehicle. She watched the St. George's fort pass-by in their right. She remembered a visit to the fort with her ex-boyfriend Vishal, a couple of months ago. The famous Anna Memorial and the MGR memorial passed-by in their left, followed by the Marina beach and the Gandhi beach. Their car drove fast for half an hour cutting through traffic, occasionally halting at red lights.

Piyu also watched the magnificent Marundeeswarar Temple, which was a very popular religious spot in Chennai. People believe that by consuming the mixture of sacred ashes, milk, and water offered here in the temple of Marundeeswarar – god of medicine – can cure even the most serious of illnesses. She bowed her head slightly in reverence and to offer a silent prayer.

It was then when Piyu sensed that something was wrong there. As far as she knew, they had already left the police headquarters behind them. They were speeding on the East Coast road, which was undoubtedly in the opposite direction. She couldn't resist and asked, "Where exactly are we going? Aren't we supposed to go to the police headquarters?"

Zac and Viren turned backwards. Samar too moved his gaze to Piyu's surprised face.

"I think we are in the wrong direction," she added.

Viren, too, realized the same thing. The police headquarters was just behind the Marina beach, opposite to the Queen Mary's College, which they had left behind fifteen minutes ago.

"Sir, are you there?" Viren nudged the senior officer. He offered no response. Viren looked at the constable sitting beside him, who stared incessantly out of the black-tinted window.

"This is not right," Piyu uttered, "We need to get down. Please stop the car, sir."

Samar was too shocked to respond. He was confident that Piyu was just overreacting, but complete silence in part of the policemen caused suspicion in him also.

"Come on, stop the car," Zac spoke authoritatively. "We are not under arrest. We can come on our own to the headquarters."

Still no response.

"Okay. I'm opening the door," Zac said, almost pulling the lever of the door on his side.

With no warning, the ACP turned and aimed his gun at Zac. "You'll do no such thing," he threatened.

Zac immediately let go of the lever.

Piyu gave out a feared shriek. The ACP trained his gun on her. She instantly fell silent; her heart was beating like a rock'n'roll drum. Her eyes widened in horror as she gasped with her mouth fully open.

"Who are you?" Samar inquired, "Where are you taking us."

"I think you know the answer," the officer replied.

"You work for DK, don't you?"

The policeman kept silent.

"How did you find us? Why did you have to kill Mr. Mukherjee? Everything you needed was with us."

"It's called collateral damage."

"No," Piyu said aggressively, "Collateral damage is when one innocent gets killed while saving thousands. You killed an innocent man while planning to kill another million or even more than that. It's called fucking terrorism."

Makhija pulled the hammer of his pistol as he pointed the gun at her face.

Driven by impulse, Zac suddenly grabbed the hand of the officer and bent it upwards. The constable who sat beside Viren lunged to help the ACP and was grabbed by the neck and left hand by Viren. Samar held the other hand of the constable.

The driver pressed the accelerator straight to the floor and drove speedily onto a flyover.

Zac's muscular arms gave fierce competition to the ACP, who tried to point the gun towards his face. Zac tried to turn his gun towards the ceiling and snatch it from his hands in the meantime. The aim of the weapon hovered near Zac's face and neck. He bent sideways to move out of its line of fire, exposing Piyu directly at gunpoint.

In this ruckus, the muzzle end of the .32 colt pistol swung up and down and side-to-side, pointing alternatively at the ceiling, at the window, and at Piyu. She moved briskly from side to side to stay out of the target region of the gun. With a sudden deafening bang, the trigger got pulled, and the bullet got fired. Piyu winced, and her eyes closed instantly as her whole body shivered.

CHAPTER SIXTEEN

Two Nights Ago, DK's House

Viren, Piyu, and Zac were sitting on the bed in DK's house. More than fifteen hours had passed since Samar had been sent to Australia to fetch the things which could get them free from the grasp of the devil DK.

"I am completely exhausted," said Piyu and rested her head against the wall behind the bed.

Zac pursed his lips. His eyelids, too, were feeling heavy from lack of sleep. He was irritated.

Viren stood up and looked through the window. The sea looked calm and tranquil. He looked below; there was no one, no goons of DK guarding the rear exit. This might be the perfect opportunity, he thought. But within a while, a man came out of the bungalow onto the sand. He walked a few steps towards the sea and stopped. He lowered his hands down to his groin area and relieved himself. He shook his waist circularly as if signing on the sand with his bladder fluid.

Viren turned back and observed Piyu dozing against the wall. He moved his gaze to Zac, who too was on the verge of drifting off. He was facing the ceiling, head resting on his hands and supported against the wall.

Viren walked to the door and stepped out. He descended the stairs and entered the main hall of the bungalow. He was tired, but the anxiety didn't allow sleep to come. He was in a desperate need for a drink. Thus, he walked down to the bar and made himself a large peg of whisky with soda. He put two cubes of ice into it.

He checked from the corner of his eyes. A dark, rustic man – a hireling of DK - was taking a siesta over a stool, near the rear exit. Viren gulped down the golden liquid in one go and put down the emptied glass on the bar table. He turned to leave but stood rooted at his place. He was jolted when he recognized the person standing directly face to face with him.

Viren's face turned grey with shock. "Bhaiya!" he cried. For a fleeting moment, Viren thought Pankaj had somehow tracked them down and had come to rescue them from their ordeal. But it was far from the truth. "What are you doing here?" he interrogated.

"I…I…" Pankaj was stopped mid-sentence by DK from behind.

"He works for me," DK spoke as he joined the two brothers, "And to say the least, he has proved to be a great asset for me so far."

Viren was stupefied from the revelation. It suddenly occurred to him that it must be Pankaj who had aided DK, who so far couldn't trace Samar but got to him as soon as he entered the country after so many years.

Pankaj had come to Chennai seven years ago to work as an insurance agent. He was brought here from New Delhi by his childhood friend, who worked here as an administrative officer in an insurance company. He had promised a permanent job in the company once Pankaj had gained some experience in the field. Almost three years had passed; Pankaj kept working as an agent with no guaranteed income. He was an ambitious young man. He never feared to dream big. But his sky-high dreams and punctuated income from selling insurance policies had him end up working for DK.

He was acquainted with DK's pursuit for the owner of that Villa near the Trinity church that happened to be in the neighbourhood of him. When he was familiarized with the fact that Samar was the sole living owner of the house, he had called DK instantly. He conveyed him all the information that he had gathered from his brother about this parentless young businessman. DK conducted further research about Samar and realized that Naman – the only son of Jaswant Oza – was christened as Samar and sent to his uncle, who lived in Melbourne.

"I can't believe you work for this fuckhead," Viren yelled at his brother, "It means all these years you lied to us."

"I'm sorry, brother. I had no choice," said Pankaj.

"You always have a choice, brother."

"Not in this country, Viren. I realized it a long time ago that you can't be happy and nice both at the same time here. I had tried everything to succeed here, but nothing happened," there was a sense of desperation in Pankaj's voice. "At each and every turn, I was oppressed and taken advantage of. I worked hard, so hard that I started eating only once a day. But years of hard work didn't take me anywhere. But now," he paused to look at his little brother's disgusted face, "Now I have everything."

"And it's just starting," DK added, "I have so many things in my mind for you two brothers. Only the sky is the limit."

Viren stood silently, looking at his brother's face. He felt sadder as he didn't even find the slightest hint of guilt in Pankaj's eyes. He shook his head in despair and spoke finally, "You stink, brother. I still remember you as the one who had beaten me and refused to talk to me for days since I was caught cheating in exams. You were my teacher, my mentor, my best friend. I looked up to you whenever I needed help. But now I feel ashamed about even calling you my brother."

"I am still your best friend, buddy. But I had some responsibilities too. You were still in college, and daddy had retired already. His meagre pension was insufficient even to support his own medical needs. Mother would call me every two days, asking me to send some money. They never let you realize what we were going through at that time so that you could study whole-heartedly. I was so proud of you when you took up engineering. I was dying to see you graduate from college. But until then, I had to support the family, and I could see no choice but to join this man. I know I have failed you. But I had my own reasons, and they were justified."

Viren shook his head and started walking towards the staircase to join Zac and Piyu upstairs.

Pankaj stopped his brother mid-way. He held his arm and took him away from DK. "You have to listen to me," he whispered.

Viren jerked his arm free from his brother's grip.

"You don't understand. These people are too dangerous. They know where we live. If we don't cooperate, they will not blink twice before killing us two and our parents."

"Why did you have to tell him about Samar in the first place?" Hadn't you done that, none of us would have been in this predicament? You betrayed me and my friends," Viren replied bitterly.

"I am sorry, okay, I am really sorry. But just think about this, who are you fighting for? Those people whom you didn't even know a few days ago?"

"They're my friends now," Viren snapped.

"Okay, fine. They are your friends, and you love them, let's say. But what DK want is very clear. He wants that vaccine. Once he gets that, everyone is free to live happily. We don't know if your friend is ready to cooperate or not, be whatever his reasons. That's why we want you to keep an eye on him and let us know if he is playing smart. DK has promised nobody will get hurt if everyone plays by his rules. So I am just suggesting that you make sure your friend Samar cooperates fully. DK gets the cure. He makes billions of money or gives it away, we couldn't care less. Anyway, many people can be saved with that. We and our loved ones will be saved, however."

Viren looked at his feet and then at his brother's face. He kept mum and walked straight upstairs. He entered the room where Zac and Piyu were kept. He looked at Piyu, who had now spread herself along the edge of the bed and was sleeping peacefully.

"Where were you?" Zac demanded as he stood crossed-arm by the floor-to-ceiling window and observed the sea-waves breaking on the shore.

"Downstairs, to get a drink. Can't bear the anxiety," replied Viren.

"There are still many hours for Sam to return. Wanna catch some sleep?"

"Can't really sleep. My head is throbbing like a frog."

"I still don't know if Sam will give that thing to that old rotting shithead so easily. I hope he makes the best decision. He always takes the best decision. He's a genius in this matter," Zac praised his childhood friend.

"I hope he does," Viren replied absent-mindedly, "A lot of things are on stakes, and only he decides everyone's fate." He crossed his arms and stood silently, watching the faint light coming from a distant ship on the horizon.

Next night, Viren was sitting with Samar at Mukherjee's house. Mr. Mukherjee had offered a drink, which he refused and moved upstairs to the guestroom allocated for his stay for the night. He was looking through some wall pictures featuring Muskaan with her parents. His eyes caught Piyu sitting on the parapet of the balcony of the adjacent room, where Piyu was staying. It was raining heavily. She spoke to Zac enthusiastically, who stood in front of her, smiling and watching deep into her eyes.

Viren first met Piyu at the office of Beyond Horizon. She had come for a summer internship, and Viren was her mentor. Piyu was very enthusiastic about work. She was intelligent and dynamic. Viren really admired her excellence in manipulating numbers. He soon developed a crush for her. He had asked her for lunch a couple of times, which she never refused. They were getting closed until one day she came up with her boyfriend on a visit to the Marina beach. Viren's heart shrank to the size of a peanut. He suppressed his feelings with tremendous efforts. He never let his face tell the story of his heart. Say it love or infatuation, he masked it with a smile of friendship.

A sudden shrill from Piyu broke the steady enchanting rhythm of the rain falling on the leaves of the tall coconut trees. She was dangling upside down by the railing, and Zac had grabbed her legs to keep her from falling. Big drops of rainwater dropped from the leaves above, kissing Piyu's forehead on their way down to the ground a decametre below.

Viren ran fast to the other room to help Piyu. By the time he entered the room, Zac had managed to pull her up. She hugged him tightly and kissed on his neck. "I love you, Zac," he heard her saying.

Viren left quietly. He walked along the hallway. He passed his guestroom and walked to the end. A landline telephone was kept on a circular wooden table. He picked the receiver and dialled the numbers. "Hello…" he said into the phone.

CHAPTER SEVENTEEN

Piyu opened her eyes. She had heard a gunshot and closed her eyes, shaken by the loud bang. She noticed a bullet hole in the collar of Zac's shirt. The bullet had passed through his collar before penetrating through the rear window. The glass broke into crumbs and fell onto the street behind.

Zac put more effort this time, managing to turn the gun halfway towards the ACP. The trigger got pulled once again. The bullet hit something, and this time, it was the driver, the middle-aged constable. It entered the back of his skull and made an exit through his forehead. The blood pushed out through the hole and spread across the windshield. The driver fell forward on the steering wheel. The dead-weight of his foot pushed the accelerator down right to the floor.

The black SUV sped fast on the relatively empty afternoon roads of Chennai outskirts. It ran on a flyover when the dead constable's body slipped over the steering, rotating the steering wheel half-round to the left. The SUV swerved hard and hit the side wall of the flyover before it flipped over the railing. Just before the car was about to fall on the other side of the wall, Zac opened the door on his side and jumped out. He was followed by Viren. The ACP tried to open the door on his side, but it was stuck by the impact.

Samar and Piyu were stuck in the rear of the vehicle and couldn't do much to save themselves. However, a big bump threw Samar upwards and then halfway out through the broken rear window. He grabbed the railing of the wall and pulled himself out just in time.

Piyu couldn't react fast and went along the car, which fell engine-first on the road several metres below. The impact broke the windshield into crumbs and crushed the ACP's neck. His crumpled body lay lifeless in the upside-down car, braced by the seatbelt.

The boys started to run, as soon as they got their bearings, to help Piyu. Their minds had gone numb by the series of sudden atrocious events. They came running to the car which by now had caught fire. A crowd gathered near the scene. Zac was hoping against all hopes, but he knew that the fall was fatal enough. He could see, through the broken rear window, the inanimate form of Piyu lying on the ceiling of the inverted car. Samar and Viren tried to enter the vehicle. The rear of the car was squashed by the slam; it was impossible to enter it from behind. They hoped Piyu had survived the blow.

Viren opened the middle door of the car. He found the other constable who was sitting adjacent to him earlier, lying motionless and soaked in blood. He checked his pulse. There was life, but definitely not for long. He pulled the bloody, half-dead cop out of the car and placed him on the road far from it.

Zac crawled into the vehicle from the middle door. Viren circled around it and entered through the door on the opposite side. They tried together to get Piyu out of the car, but couldn't reach her between the seats and the crushed ceiling. The fire, which by now crawled up to the front seats, didn't help either.

Meanwhile, Samar, along with some of the gathered people, tried blowing the fire out with sand, water, and whatever they got their hands on.

Zac finally reached Piyu and put all his strength to pull her but couldn't. Viren too tried hard to get her out but couldn't move her more than even a few inches. They saw blood coming out of Piyu's shoulder and head and knew that time was crucial. They noticed that Piyu's belt was stuck on a metal rod, which didn't let them pull her forward. The fabric of the front seat burnt furiously, and the flame was caught up by Viren's shirt. His arm burnt, and he was forced to make his way out.

The fire had reached Zac's face too. Samar and Viren knew it was too late. They couldn't save Piyu, but they had to save Zac. They caught his legs and started pulling him out.

Zac didn't lose hope, just as yet. He kept trying. He kicked his friends hard and crawled further into the car until he reached Piyu's waist. He pushed her inwards so that her belt would release the rod. Once he got her free, he grabbed her from shoulders and shouted to his friends outside, *"Pull! Now!"*

Zac was pulled out quickly by his friends, with Piyu along. They finally got both of them out of the car, which by now started burning furiously.

Zac carried Piyu in arms to the ambulance that had recently entered the scene. Someone from the crowd had called the emergency hotline for ambulance and fire brigade.

The medical attendants put unconscious but still-alive Piyu and the constable into the ambulance. The boys accompanied them, and the ambulance rode fast towards the hospital a few miles away.

CHAPTER EIGHTEEN

"She should be fine now," said the doctor as soon as he came out of the operation theatre. Zac was standing right in front of the door the whole time, waiting for someone to come out and assure him that she would be fine. When the red light above the door had gone off, his heart started pounding against his ribs. When the doctor came out, Zac almost pulled him towards himself as if threatening him to say only what he wanted to hear. Luckily, for the doctor, he did not have to lie to save himself.

"Can we see her, doctor?" asked Samar.

"She is in a state of induced unconscious right now. We are shifting her to ICU, you can see her after that. But no more than two persons at a time."

"How much time will it take for her to recover completely?" asked Viren.

"She had several injuries on her head, shoulder, and legs, but fortunately, nothing was too deep. She had passed out before the impact, which actually worked in her favour. A tensed body is more prone to damages than a relaxed body. There are a couple of fractures in the skull and ribs, which will take a few months. Except that, everything is superficial and should be all gone in a fortnight."

"Thank you, doctor, thank you so much," Zac said and hugged the doctor.

Half an hour later, Piyu was shifted to the ICU. Zac waited until the nurse gave them a green flag to enter the ICU. He half-walked-half-ran into the ICU to find a still-unconscious Piyu lying bandaged on the hospital bed. He was followed by Samar. They watched Piyu as she took deep breaths through the breathing mask attached to her face. There were all types of medical equipment attached to her body via sensors, monitoring all her vital signs.

Zac touched Piyu's fingers and slowly took her hand in his. The motionless, enervated frame of Piyu lying on that hospital bed was the polar opposite to the girl who was energetic, dynamic and full of life, whom he loved more than anything, whom he desired more than anything. But it didn't lessen his love for her even for a driblet. He held her hand tight, and a drop of tear welled up in his eyes.

All this while, Samar was watching his friend intently from the opposite side. He was watching each and every emotion surfacing on Zac's face and knew instantly what he was seeing. It was love, in its purest form. He had noticed Zac losing himself in Piyu's eyes right on that night when he introduced him to her at that party. He had known Zac long enough to know that it was not like another young age infatuation that comes and goes in a blink of an eye but was something more profound. He watched in awe when Zac put his life on the line to save Piyu from that flaming car. When Zac caught him staring, he gave a warm, consoling smile to his friend.

Meanwhile, Viren sat in front of the ICU, staring at his foot. He knew that he had goofed up big time. Everything that had gone wrong was due to his misplaced trust and poor judgement. It was he who informed DK about Mr. Mukherjee and his involvement with them. It was he who brought death to the old couple and suffering to their granddaughter. It was he who was responsible for the misery of Samar, Zac, and especially Piyu, who took him as a friend. He knew that DK is not going to leave their trail just as yet. He had to act smart. The stakes had risen. Apart from the lives of his and his friends, lives of million others now came into the equation, who could die from that deadly virus waiting in that red package to be reborn and unleash hell.

He stood up and turned to leave, but stopped on his track when he saw Pankaj approaching him. He looked at his brother and cried on top of his voice, "go away and die Pankaj before I kill you myself." Few nurses turned and gave him a scolding look.

"Brother! Please listen to me first," begged Pankaj.

"I don't want to listen; I don't even want to see your face. You disgust me. And if there's any humanity left inside you, go and get lost forever and free this world of your burden," Viren rebuked sharply.

"Please, brother."

Viren shook his head and walked past him.

"DK has our parents, Viren," Pankaj disclosed. Viren stopped rooted to the ground. "He wanted me to kill you and your friends and get that key. When I protested, he kidnapped our parents. He wants you to persuade your friends for handing the key to him and forget all about this."

"I can't do that. They will not listen to me," Viren replied.

"Then send them to DK, he will extract what he wants, and I promise there will be no bloodshed. We can treat all of this as a shared nightmare, which never happened in reality," Pankaj said.

"And what about those million people who will die from that virus. Who knows if we will be the one who dies first from it?" Viren demanded.

"That thing is just non-sense. No one is going to use it ever since it will mean complete destruction. It is meant only for holding the rein of absolute power. And whoever holds power, how does it affect middle-class people like us? We need to save what we got, and what we got is only us and the people we love. And what do you think, if DK intended couldn't he come himself and get whatever he wanted. But that would've only meant death for all. He is giving us this chance for my sake only."

Viren stood silently for a long time. He looked everywhere but in his brother's eyes. Finally, when he did, he said, "Promise me there will be no bloodshed. I want mom, dad, and all my friends alive and unscathed."

"I promise you. Trust me?" said Pankaj.

"I do, for the last time," replied Viren.

It had been little over half an hour since Zac and Samar had entered ICU. In the meantime, Pankaj had left as unannounced as he came, leaving Viren lost deep in his thoughts. He was sweating profusely and was unsure of everything. He knew he had an important task in hand but had no idea how he would do it. He couldn't possibly let his friends become aware of his intentions. He would never be able to persuade them according to his wish, that he knew.

"Is she okay? Is she conscious yet?" Viren inquired.

"No. Not yet," replied Samar.

"What's next?" Viren asked again.

"I have no idea right now. We can't even go to the police," Samar spoke despairingly.

"I think you should leave the country as soon as possible," suggested Viren.

"But our passports are with that bastard," Zac roared.

"I know someone who can help us. There's a friend of mine who can get you a fake passport and can also ferry you out of the country safely," said Viren.

"Where can we meet him?" asked Samar.

"We go to the docks and ask for Rasan. He can be very choosy and has a good appetite for money."

"But, we are out of money completely."

"I said he's a friend of mine," Viren winked and added, "He'll charge me double later, but for the time being, he's the only person who can get us out of this mess. But who will stay with Piyu?"

"Zac can stay with her," replied Samar.

Zac snapped out of his reverie. He was constantly worried about Piyu and had missed most part of the conversation, but had had enough to know what they were planning to do. "Are you sure?" he asked.

"Yes, buddy. You are needed more here than there with us," said Samar.

"Okay, let me make a quick call from the PCO. I have to inform Rasan about our arrival," Viren said and walked past.

CHAPTER NINETEEN

Chennai Port

Viren walked deeper into the enormous shipping warehouse. More than two dozen cargos were lying tightly sealed and ready to be shipped. He looked upwards; the ceiling of the warehouse was intimidatingly high. Just below the slanted rooftop, a large steel hook dangled from the gantry girder. He moved his gaze downwards to look at the operator cabin in the hope of finding someone there in flesh and blood. There was not a single soul in the gigantic place.

Viren looked over his shoulder to find Samar, who stood behind him as disoriented and confused as himself. They were standing inside a warehouse of a local shipping company. The vast area that the building covered looked as if it belonged to a big, successful company that never ran out of jobs. The hundreds of metre length of the rectangular place was staggering, and the end appeared to be beyond the horizon. The grave-like state of the site was but counter-intuitive.

Samar checked his watch to see if they were early. They weren't. "Are you sure this is the place?" he inquired.

Viren nodded.

"Where's your man?" he asked again.

Viren shrugged but didn't look back.

Samar eyed Viren deliberately, scrutinizing the sudden mysterious demeanour of his friend. His guts told him something was wrong. He came forward and put a hand on Viren's shoulder just as the metallic shutter roared open across the warehouse. The brilliant rays of sunlight from outside obscured the figures that entered through the opening. Samar watched silhouettes of three men approaching them, taking slow, determined steps. He looked at Viren.

Viren's face contorted as his eyes adjusted to the brightness.

Samar waited till the shadows came closer, and their face became discernible. He was expecting a black Tamil man probably short with a rustic appearance, wearing torn-up clothes, and chewing tobacco. But what he saw was horrendous, as if he saw a dead man walking. The man in the middle was none other than DK.

"Run," he whispered in Viren's ears and turned to run. He stood rooted to the ground when two men entered through the door behind him and pulled down the shutter. He turned back and faced DK.

"What do you want, DK?" Samar yelled furiously.

"I want what you stole from me," DK replied.

"It was never yours. I stole nothing from you."

"The research always belonged to DRL," DK snapped. He took a step closer to Samar and shouted out loudly, "And *I* am the owner of that fucking lab."

"You are nothing but a fucking scumbag, you old man. You will kill everyone on this earth, and I will never let you do so."

DK laughed out hysterically. "You are just like Jaswant - brave-hearted, but sometimes too stupid to understand the risks," he said and gestured his men. Two of them held Samar from shoulders, and others searched him top to bottom. Samar tried to set himself free but was overpowered by the four gym-trained muscular men. The goons recovered the blue package and the weird metallic key from the pocket of his jacket.

DK held the key and observed it. "Now, the password, please?"

"Shove it in your ass and go to hell where you belong," Samar snapped.

DK smiled, "As I said brave but stupid." He stretched his hand towards Viren.

Viren took the key and started rotating the dials. He entered the numbers in the proper sequence. After he set the last dial to its right position, he pushed the top and it clicked.

"There you go," DK clapped.

He almost snatched the key from Viren's hand and walked to the nearby table.

Samar looked at Viren in exasperation. "Why?" he asked.

"I am sorry," Viren uttered teary-eyed, "My parents are with him."

Samar understood instantly that Viren did what he had to do. It must've been a tough choice for him.

DK's men placed the locker, which they had stolen from Mr. Mukherjee's house, on the table. He tried to insert the key into the keyhole in all angles before it finally got through the hole. He rotated it almost a full-circle, and the door of the locker finally clicked open. He looked into the locker and took out an opaque brown conical flask, corked snugly. He held it high as a trophy. He put it down on the table and put the two packages beside it. His treasure was complete. He was exhilarated by the fact that his twenty-year-long chase had finally ended. Except for a final hitch, which soon will be taken care of. He gestured his men.

DK's men got hold of Samar and Viren. "Move," one of them yelled.

"What is this, DK?" Viren shouted, "You promised."

"Sorry, my friend. You know too much. And to quote a great man 'Knowledge is dangerous.'"

The goons pushed Viren and Samar towards the sea.

"At least let my parents live. They know nothing," Viren cried.

"I can't say for sure. You know, I am not good at keeping promises," DK said smugly, revelling in his own merriment. The air around him was filled with joy - the joy of victory - thick enough to cloud his senses, thick enough to keep him from noticing the sounds coming from outside.

"I shouldn't have trusted you," yelled Viren.

"Yes, you shouldn't," DK replied.

"That's why I didn't," Viren got DK's attention.

DK turned to look at him. Suddenly, all the shutters got pulled up. Dozens of men entered the premises and swarmed around the whole place.

"Intelligence Bureau!! Put your hands up," one of the officers commanded.

Two of DK's men were fool enough and pulled out their guns by instinct and got shot instantaneously. DK, too tried to flee with the packages and the flask. In his desperate attempt, he got tipped over one of his own man's corpse and fell. He managed to save the solution and the blue package, but the red one fell and struck hard against the floor. In an instant the flat cuboidal box in red exploded. And with it exploded a potential threat to the whole humanity. DK watched in horror. He gave out a deep sigh and lay on the floor with his hands wide open. Two officers approached him and cuffed his hands.

One of the officers walked to Viren and shook his hands, "Rajeev Menon – Assistant Central Intelligence Officer. Thank you for your help."

"My parents?" Viren asked.

"Our team raided DK's bungalow and arrested five men. But we couldn't find your parents. I am sure we will find them after we interrogate DK and his men."

Viren eyed DK, who was being dragged by the officers. DK looked back at him, "This doesn't end here," he uttered mischievously.

Samar placed a hand on Viren's shoulder in an assuring manner.

Viren turned to the ACP, "Did you find my brother?"

"No. We tried to triangulate his number. But it was unreachable. The last signal it caught was from DK's house four hours ago. We have released an arrest warrant for him too."

Viren nodded slightly.

CHAPTER TWENTY

Piyu woke up in the hospital. She was happy to find all her friends safe and sound, standing by her bed. "Are you people alright?" she spoke meekly.

"Yes, we are," Samar replied, "How are you feeling?"

"Tired," she grimaced.

"Must be the sedatives," Zac looked into Piyu's eyes and fought a great urge to kiss her. Although she was at her worst, he found her no less beautiful than ever.

Piyu looked in Zac's eyes. She was sure she spotted a tear in his eyes, but Zac was too strong to let his emotions overcome him. "What did I miss? The last thing I remember is we were in a police car."

"The police were with DK. We were being kidnapped," Viren explained.

"But why, how?" Piyu mumbled.

"For the moment," Sam intervened, "let us not overwhelm you with the details. All you need to know is the matter is in the hands of professionals, and we all are out of danger. Except..."

"Except?" asked Piyu.

"Except that Viren's parents were taken hostage by DK and are now missing."

Piyu looked into Viren's eyes. There were tears; tears of sorrow and helplessness. She held his hand.

"Please excuse me," Viren freed his hand and walked towards the door.

"Where are you going," asked Samar.

"To the police, let me see if they found anything about my parents."

"Let me come with you," Samar offered.

"No, please. I have called some of my friends for help. You guys should stay here with Piyu. I'll be back in few hours," Viren replied gloomily.

"You sure?" Samar asked.

Viren nodded and left.

After waiting for hours at the police station in the hope of getting his parents' whereabouts, Viren left dejected towards his home. He fished his keys out of his pockets and tried to open the front door. To his surprise, it was open but bolted from inside. He rang the doorbell.

He couldn't believe his eyes when he saw his mother open the door.

"Ma! Are you alright? What had happened? Where is Papa?" Viren was exhilarated.

"Beta! I am alright, and Papa is inside. But we are concerned about Pankaj," Viren's mother said in a grievous tone.

"What happened? Where is Pankaj?" asked Viren.

Viren listened carefully as his parents unveiled the series of events that took place a few hours ago. They told him how Pankaj's friends came and started misbehaving with them. How his friends forced them to go along on the gunpoint. They couldn't recall much of the details as they were blindfolded. Only when Pankaj removed their blindfolds after what seemed like an eternity, they could see that they were held in a small, dark room. There was no window, only a single door at the far side from where they sat on steel chairs with their limbs tied behind their back. Pankaj was anxious. He had a knife with which he untied them and escorted them outside. He asked them to go straight to their home and wait for him.

Viren was furious at his brother in his own right. He swore at that moment that he will never see his face in his lifetime. Less did he know that he will have to, very next day and for the very last time. Less did he know that before rescuing their parents, Pankaj had fought with three of his goons. Less did he know that he was shot twice in the mid-rift. In the heat of the moment, partly due to the lack of visibility, his parents missed the blood that soaked his t-shirt when he freed them. Viren loved his brother, but he couldn't get into his mind ever. Pankaj was reserved and contented in his own little world. He sold his soul to a devil, so Viren could complete his engineering. Now he was too deep into the hole to come out ever again. But he was happy for his brother. He wanted his brother to realize his dreams for both of them, to achieve what he couldn't, to reach where he couldn't. He wanted to see his brother at the pinnacle, but now he couldn't.

Samar looked at the board of the small little shop. "SBJ computers and cyber café," it said.

He asked for a computer with the internet. Promptly, he was escorted to a 3x3 cubicle with a machine that looked older than him, one with a CRT monitor and a keyboard probably bulkier than the wooden chair. However, he didn't complain as it will serve his purpose. He didn't need much time with it anyway.

He quickly started the pc and opened Skype in it. He fished out a small piece of paper from his wallet and looked at the text. He remembered the moment under that coconut tree with Mr. Mukherjee that now seemed like a lifetime ago. During their conversation, Mr. Mukherjee had said, "See Samar, I want you to keep this with you." He gave him a small piece of paper that he took out from his little pocket diary. Something was written on it. "What is it?" Samar had asked. "Once the dust settles and you are safe at your home, I want you to contact someone. He may give you more information on your father than I can."

Mr. Mukherjee's voice reverberated in his mind, *He may give you more information on your father.* Samar was impatient. *Safe and Sound my ass,* he thought as he entered the skype id of his contact – phil_58.

Samar was glad to see that his contact was online at the moment. He adjusted the webcam and put the headphone on his head. He clicked on the little camera button beside his contact's name. He waited for the other party to accept the call. Once he did, it took Samar a moment to register what he saw on the screen. He was stunned to the core, sweating profusely, his eyes broadened like a lamb under the blade. *How on earth,* he wondered. He felt as if the earth cracked open right beneath his feet. He was so dizzy he thought he would fall from the chair. He looked at the walls of the tiny cubicle that appeared smaller than before.

Finally, once he absorbed the shock to a degree to which that kind of shock could be absorbed anyway, he muttered under his breath, "Dad?"

CHAPTER TWENTY-ONE

Twenty Years Ago

"Mo...oom!!! Let's go, dad's waiting," Naman cried from the front gate.

It was a breezy Sunday morning in January, Naman was excited to go on a picnic with his parents. Once a month, his father would take him and his mother to Mukherjee's. Mukherjee was a childhood friend of Naman's father. They were inseparable when young, as they are now. From there, they would head straight to the beach. The men would take the boat for hours into the ocean for fishing, while the women would chat and discuss their recent predicaments about how their husbands would not listen to them, how their kids were getting naughtier day by day.

"Coming beta! Let me pack the lunch, or what will we eat in the afternoon," Naman's mother yelled back. Naman's mother, Archana Oza, a beautiful young lady in her mid-thirties, was a school teacher before marriage. Even after her marriage with Jaswant Oza, she would give private tuitions to school kids. After Naman was born, she took the full-time job of a mother. Hailing from Rajasthan, she was a sweet woman, happily devoted to her family. Although their marriage was an arranged one, Archana and Jaswant were head over heels now in love with each other. More than that, they loved their kid as deeply as the ocean.

"Oh, dad! Mom is going to take another hour it seems," annoyed Naman said to his father and grumpily took the front seat in their six-year-old cherry-red Maruti 800. His fair, bubbly face all sweaty and red due to repeatedly running back and forth to the house for the fourth time. His bold, stuffy lips curved in a pout in anger. Naman was seven, and exquisitely handsome. His bright eyes and long lashes that he took from his father, added charm to his boyish cuteness.

Whenever his father would ask what he would become once he's an adult, Naman's replies were always different. Sometimes doctor was what he would say, sometimes astronaut, and another time he would like to become a pilot. But one day, when his father asked the same question, Naman said he would become a businessman like his uncle Naresh. Since that day, his answer was consistent. He was a good kid. Brilliant in studies, fierce in sports, sociable and polite - the dream of any parent. Jaswant and Archana couldn't be prouder.

Naman was fiddling with the side mirror when finally, after what seemed to him like an eternity, his mother came and took the backseat.

It was only half an hour's drive to Mukherjee's home. Mukherjee, a psychiatrist by profession, lived with his son and wife in a big bungalow in the east Chennai near Marina beach. His bungalow was an old rugged building with a small lawn in the front and with two coconut trees shading it from the blazing Chennai sun in the afternoons.

Adhusudhan Mukherjee's wife, Sujata Mukherjee, in her late thirties, was a pleasant woman. They met in a Durga Puja ceremony in Calcutta, she came with her friends and Adhusudhan was with his cousins. They were introduced by one of his cousins, who were schrool mates with Sujata. Adhusudhan was twenty-four at that time, had just completed his studies. Sujata was twenty-six. Their marriage was opposed by both of their families due to their age. The bride being older than the groom was a big taboo in Indian culture during those times. However, after months' protest from both of them, they were married in a traditional Bengali-style wedding with lots of sweets and fishes.

Mukherjee's son Parthak, who was five years older than Naman, was a shy and reserved kid. He was brilliant in studies, always topped his class. He wore a pair of round, heavy glasses with a strap around his neck, which looked too childish on a pre-teen like him. His hair drenched with coconut oil his mother put in his hair every morning, parting it sidewise. Naman and Parthak didn't get along much, partly due to their age difference, but mostly due to their character difference.

After a full day of fun and excitement at the beach, Naman was exhausted and slept in the car. His father took him on his shoulder and carefully rested him on the bed. His mother removed his shoes and pulled the sheet over him. She noticed a smile on his face. It was an enjoyable day for Samar. He was excited for the next day when he would tell his friends that he caught six fishes from the ocean, his biggest catch being a 1.5 kg mackerel.

Jaswant was quietly sitting on the couch, browsing through a scientific magazine when his telephone rang. It was nine at night. He knew who it was. His childhood friend Guru always called on Sundays to catch up. Although they taught in the same university, they could only talk to each other over the telephone. Due to their busy schedule in their respective academic and research work, they would meet once in a fortnight for a drink outside the campus. Apart from that, their weekly phone call was the only means of catching up.

"Hi, Guru! I was expecting your call," Jaswant said in a cheering tone.

"How was your picnic?"

"Good…good. Naman really enjoyed it. Talked to Mukherjee recently?"

"Yeah, talked to him a couple of days ago. How's your research going?"

"Glad you mentioned," Jaswant said like an enthusiastic kid, "It's working. The formula is stable enough in the room temperature for any practical use. Normal vibrations and day to day movements do not have any influence on the product. Even in an elevated temperature of 80°C, the product doesn't catch fire and burst into flames, unlike earlier."

"That's great news. So what's left then?"

"It's under accelerated age test right now to check its stability fifty years after production. It will be useless if it degrades by itself with age. So far, results have been optimistic. It'll take another month, then I'll file the patents."

"That's exciting, my friend. Your research is brilliant. It will give data encryption another meaning. Army, Intelligence, Police, everyone will be head over heels to buy your research."

"Oh, come on! It's nothing compared to your work. Your research will save lives. A cure to HIV! That'll be the next big thing in medical history after penicillin. How's it going, by the way?" asked Jaswant.

"It's going great. The new candidate looks promising, results are good."

"How many days since infection?"

"Fifteen"

"Still under control?"

"Looks so," Guru said diplomatically. "However, it's too early to tell."

"Ok, keep me updated. I'll probably come to your lab someday, to see your research," said Jaswant.

"You are most welcome, my friend."

"Next week?"

"Sure."

"Okay then, see you later."

"Okay. Bye."

"Bye."

Five Days Later,
Delta Research Laboratory

Jaswant was escorted by a peon to the quarantine section of the lab. The peon opened the large steel door and entered inside. Jaswant followed. The room was expansive. The blinding bright lights reflected from pure white painted walls forced him to squint his eyes while they adapted to the brightness.

Once his eyes adjusted to the light, he noticed that the room was divided into many cells. Each cell had one heavy steel door and a large glass window from top to the middle. He followed the peon to the third cell and found Gurudutt Gowda reading a book on a wooden chair.

The cell was only large enough to accommodate a single bed, a chair, and a small table. It was fully air-proof except for a small vent for the supply of purified air after passing through an electric precipitator. It ensured that no air-suspended particle or micro-organism could get in or out of the room.

Gowda was totally submerged in his book. After the peon left, Jaswant knocked on the glass window to make his friend aware of his presence. Gowda looked up from his book and smiled.

He quickly came to the window and spoke, "Oh, Jaswant! I am glad you came." His voice came through the speaker that was attached in the middle of the window.

"When you told me that they locked you in a cell, you were so mysterious I was petrified," Jaswant replied

"It's so boring here. There's nothing to do. I thought you'd like to give me some company."

"I do. But….anyways. What happened here? Why are you in quarantine?" asked Jaswant curiously.

"It's awful," Gowda's expression was suddenly grim.

"What's wrong?"

"The vaccine we were testing for last few weeks, it failed, it failed grandly," Gowda spoke exasperatedly. "You should have seen the subjects."

"Why? What happened?"

"All eight subjects were stable and showed promising results. But only until Tuesday. It was the seventeenth day of the trial. It was Tina, a female macaque, she was well in the morning. The keepers noticed some laziness in her activities. She was sitting idle for many hours, it was abnormal but nothing too serious to be concerned about. So, the keepers also didn't report anything to us. By two in the afternoon, she was lying on the floor of the cage. Her breathing was shallow and irregular. We noted her symptoms and decided to keep her in isolation. She was put in a separate cage and allowed to rest. I asked my assistant Devdutt to check on her every hour. By the next hour, she was bleeding through her eyes, nose, and anus. By 4 pm, her body had decayed. Her ribs were visible, her neck was twisted backwards in an unnatural angle. She was long dead. It was unusual. Her body was necrotized. It seemed like she was dead for a week and was left there to rot. But she was not. She was very much alive a few hours ago."

"What happened to the other subjects?"

"The other subjects," Gowda started in a sad voice. "By midnight, all of the other seven subjects showed similar symptoms. Fatigue, loss of appetite, followed by death with necrosis."

"My God," Jaswant spoke appalled by the narration of the horrific incident.

"That's not it, my friend! Something more interesting happened on the next day. After all of our eight subjects had died. Their carcasses were being prepared for the burial as per standard protocol. By noon, the keepers called us into the zoology section. What we saw was beyond our comprehension. The other six apes who were in the zoo also started showing similar symptoms as Tina. They were not even subjected to any kind of trial. Yet they had contracted the disease that killed Tina and the other apes."

"How's that even possible?" asked Jaswant.

"That's what baffled us all."

"You once mentioned that the vaccine you are developing is itself a virus and fights with HIV when infected," Jaswant tried his theory.

"Yes, you are right. It is a modified HIV strain that infects the human immune cells just like normal HIV, but it doesn't kill it. It stays idle inside until the cell is infected by a regular HIV. It then blocks the reproduction of the killer virus, thereby hindering the propagation of the disease. Since it affects only those cells that are targeted by HIV, side effects would be minimal. Well, that was the best-case scenario."

"What was the worst-case scenario?" Jaswant asked.

"HIV mutating itself to become immune against our vaccine. They are one sneaky little bastards. They evolve so fast before you even find a way to kill them, they find a way to save themselves from it. But this…. this is a nightmare.

We will probably lose all the grants that we are getting from the government and other private parties. Nobody wants to burn a huge amount of money to devise the most gruesome manner for killing apes."

"Do you think it's possible that the modified HIV mutated itself to become airborne?"

"No, that's highly unlikely. The virus is highly vulnerable to the external environment. It requires a large number of mutations occurring in a single virion, that's one in a trillion odds."

"How will you know then?"

"My whole team is under quarantine right now. This will ensure that whatever killed those apes, will stay with us only. Once we get out, we will run some tests on the tissue sample preserved from the subjects. Only then will we be in a position to tell what caused that horror," Gowda replied.

"How long will you be here?"

"Standard protocol requires us to stay twenty-one days under quarantine following such events."

"So, for three weeks, you will be here. By the way, where is DK? Does he know about all this?"

"He is in Moscow, attending some conference. We have sent a word to him. He will be here by tomorrow."

Two days later, there was an upheaval in DRL. The two zookeepers who were responsible for caring for the animal subjects in DRL fell seriously ill. They were immediately admitted to a renowned hospital in Chennai under quarantine and 24x7 medical care.

It was early in the morning when the younger among the two keepers, Jeeva, raised the alarm. He was kept under quarantine in the quarantine room of the Delta Research Laboratory. Each of the quarantine cells had a buzzer for their occupants to call the hands if they needed anything. It took the hand less than a minute to come and find Jeeva lying on the floor in his own vomit. He was instructed strictly not to open the cells without the permission of higher authorities. He rushed to the main lab and asked the senior scientists to come and take a look.

The scientists were aghast to see the view inside the cell. They were impatient to go inside the room, but they had to follow the protocol. They quickly brought out a full-body suit of the shelf and started wearing it. The suit was specially designed to provide medical care in times of epidemics. The same type of suits was used by the WHO workers to help during the disease breakouts in Africa and other underdeveloped countries. They had already called the ambulance.

They spread a big biomedical plastic bag on the floor. It was specially designed to cover a whole human body ill with highly hazardous and contagious diseases. The bag was almost six feet in length with a zip lock. There were small openings for ventilation at every one-foot tri-axially distributed around the circumference. Those were closed with micro-filters to contain all kinds of pathogens.

It took half an hour for the paramedical personnel to drive the patient to the hospital, unloading him on a stretcher and transferring him to a special isolation room for patients with highly contagious diseases.

Dr. Ajith Vishwanathan was a medical officer who was assigned his case. Trained from All India Institute of Medical Sciences Delhi and a veteran with twenty years of experience as a specialist for infectious diseases, he was the best doctor in the whole city for this case.

But this case was nothing like Dr. Ajith had seen in his long career of medical practice. His patient had developed necrosis at multiple locations on his hands and legs. His breathing was irregular, and he was bleeding through his eyes intermittently. After getting briefed from the researchers from the DRL, he put his patient on a cocktail of multiple retroviral drugs and a heavy dose of intravenous antibiotics to prevent any opportunistic bacterial infection from being developed. Dr. Ajith was not superstitious, but this time he believed a complete miracle is what will save his patient.

Three hours later, Dr. Ajith received another patient. Another zookeeper from DRL. Similar symptoms, same mystery.

After a month of being into quarantine. Gowda was finally declared free of infection. He, along with his other staff, was put on a heavy dose of antibiotics and a combination of anti-viral drugs. The zookeepers of DRL had died within twelve hours after being admitted into the hospital. Gowda and his team of doctors and researchers were lucky that they didn't contract the disease. The most probable reason, they assumed, was their brief contact period with the apes. Still, the doctors didn't take chances and put them on a high dose of medicines.

Jaswant looked into his friend's eyes. They looked sad. The duo was sitting in a bar nearby the campus of IIT Madras. They had ordered their usual whisky with soda and banana chips.

Gowda's gaze was fixed on the ice cube floating in the golden liquid. After the tragedy, DRL was forced to shut its operation indefinitely by the ICMR. ICMR was the governing body of medical research in India. Multiple lawsuits were filed against DRL for negligence and illicit medical practices. Although Gowda was confident that all the necessary protocols were followed throughout the research, yet this incident will be a black botch on his career. He was sure no research lab will hire him anymore to carry out his research. His dream of finding a vaccine for HIV had now gone well beyond his reach.

Gowda kept swirling his glass for the ice to melt. He was looking through Jaswant as if he couldn't even see him. He didn't notice that his drink was finished already. Jaswant ordered for a refill.

"Adhusudhan was asking for you," Jaswant said to break the silence.

Gowda didn't reply.

"Guru?"

"Huh??" Gurudutt Gowda finally came out of his reverie.

"I said Adhusudhan was asking about you. He said he called you at your office, you didn't pick."

"I had classes back to back," Gowda said, still zoned out partially.

"I met your research assistant. He said you were at your room for the whole day and had asked everyone to not disturb," Jaswant said non-accusingly.

"Yeah! I was swamped with work actually, working on something important," Gowda felt annoyed. He was in no mood for a chat.

Jaswant sensed the irritability in his friend's demeanour. He noticed that Gowda's glass was empty, again. "Should I call for another round?"

Gowda looked into his eyes and nodded slightly. Once his glass was refilled, he took a sip and kept his glass on the table. Suddenly, he stood up and started to walk.

"Wait! Where are you going?" Jaswant enquired.

"Something important came up. I have to leave now."

"Okay! I am coming with you," Jaswant kept the cash under the glass with almost 100% tip and followed his friend.

Gowda was already out.

"Where are we going?" Jaswant asked once they flagged down a taxi and occupied the back seat.

"DRL," Gowda replied promptly.

Jaswant was reading a magazine. It was ten 'o clock in the night. Naman and his mother had gone to bed. Suddenly, the doorbell rang.

"Guru?" he took a long look at his friend. "Come inside," he let Gowda in.

Guru sat on the sofa, put his eye-glasses on the glass table in front, and sat back with his head resting on the back.

"I am pretty sure we decided on lunch. Didn't we? Why did you bailout?"

After a long pause, Gowda finally spoke, "I think I have found the answer."

"You mean you finally understood what killed those apes?" Jaswant asked precariously.

"Yes."

Jaswant waited for his friend to elaborate.

Gowda started, "You remember I told you HIV can't become airborne."

"Yes. Since they are weak and vulnerable outside the body of the host," replied Jaswant.

"Yes, they are. That's why it's difficult for them to survive the transmission from one host to another by the air route. Unless…"

"Unless?"

"Unless they get a shield for themselves."

"What kind of shield are you talking about," Jaswant asked with confusion.

"It seems the virus got a friend to help him out of his prison."

Jaswant frowned in a lack of words.

"It seems the virus mutated to infect another organism already present in the apes, probably in Tina. It was one specific, spore-forming bacteria. There have been studies on a special class of viruses called bacteriophages, which can infect bacteria. Some kill their hosts, some don't. Some change the whole biology of the host. They insert their genetic code into the DNA of the host, giving them extra new features."

"Do you think this is what happened to Tina and others? It sounds like a rare phenomenon," Jaswant guessed.

"Rare!?" Gowda growled. "It has been estimated that there can be more bacteriophages on the earth than other species combined. Ancient Indians always knew that water of river Yamuna and Ganga had some anti-bacterial properties. It was only recently that scientists have reported a high concentration of bacteriophages in the waters of Yamuna and Ganga."

"So which bacteria are we talking about? Who is this new friend of HIV?" enquired Jaswant.

"It's anthrax. I did a culture on the tissue collected from Tina. The results were confirmatory. The symptoms, too, match with those of anthrax. The only difference being anthrax is usually slow. It takes many weeks for symptoms to develop and the patient to die. That's why it's pretty much treatable. But in the case of Tina and other apes, the disease spread very fast. The only explanation is our modified virus infected the bacteria and shortened its life cycle."

"It means your research didn't fail. It's just a bad turn of events."

Gowda didn't reply.

"Come on! Cheer up. It's good news. Wait! Let me make you a drink." Jaswant stood up and walked quickly to the kitchen. He came back with two glasses of whiskey and offered one to his friend. "Did you inform this to DK yet?"

"No. Not yet." Gowda took the glass and quaffed down the golden liquid in a single gulp.

CHAPTER TWENTY-TWO

"Stop your boat now," blared the loudspeaker. It was a small interceptor craft patrolling the shores of Chennai. Assistant commandant Suryakant Pillai was the commanding officer.

As soon as a small steamboat was spotted through the telescope, the interceptor had taken a course to intercept the vehicle. It had entered the Indian territory, and its direction of travel suggested that it was coming from Jaffna, a small port city of Sri Lanka.

The boat driver stopped the boat immediately and let the coast guards come closer.

As soon as the interceptor reached the boat, a rope ladder was lowered. A young boy in his early twenties climbed down the ladder and stood on the small boat. He was followed by Pillai.

"Behenchod (sister fucker)! Where the hell do you think you are going?" asked Pillai in his usual rude and obnoxious manner.

The driver of the boat was a poor middle-aged man, weak from malnutrition. Just like most of the south-Indians and Sri Lankans, he was pitch dark. He wore a white vest torn at many places and a grey checked dhoti. "Sir…I am …" thud!! Pillai gave a hard slap to the poor fellow.

"Did I told you to speak yet?" Pillai looked at the blue tarpaulin sheet covering two-third of the deck. "What's in there?"

"It's…." thud!! Another slap.

"Did I ask you?" Pillai glared at the helpless boatman. He signalled with his eyes to subordinate to go and check.

The boy quickly removed the tarpaulin sheet and uncovered about a dozen large wooden boxes. Each box was about half a metre long and thirty-centimetre-wide and about a foot deep. The boy opened one of the boxes and was taken aback.

"Sir, these are gun parts. Kalashnikovs. At least three in each box," the boy shouted back to his boss.

"How many boxes are there?"

The boy quickly counted the boxes and replied back, "Fifteen, sir."

Pillai turned to the boatman and punched him in the face. "What is this?"

The boatman kneeled down helplessly, already bleeding from his nose. He knew he was in grave trouble. "*Sar, nan appavi, sar* (Sir, I don't know anything). I am innocent," the boatman switched from Tamil to Hindi and back again. He held Pillai's legs tightly.

The commanding officer kicked the boatman hard in the ribs, who fell on his back.

"You fucker! Don't ruin my pants," he straightened the creases in his trousers. "Your boss has paid me 2 lakhs for 10 boxes. Here we have 15. Who will pay for the rest? Your daughter? I don't think your daughter is worth so much." He turned to his junior, who shifted in his place in nervousness, not sure what to do. "Tag this boat to the shore. We will take this to our warehouse," commanded Pillai. He climbed up the rope ladder back to his vessel.

His assistant, too stunned to react, stared pitifully at the helpless boatman. Another assistant threw a steel cable from the bigger boat and shouted, "Hey! Tie this to the boat." The first assistant jolted back to reality. He quickly attached the cable to the bow of the boat and waved his hand to the second assistant.

The engine of the interceptor roared to life and started moving towards the shore. Half an hour later, it reached a bushy, isolated beach. Pillai and his two assistants climbed down on the land. He ordered his men to carry the boxes and follow him. He walked for a few yards and stood in front of a small hut. He knocked on the door three times. An old woman opened the door. She gave Pillai a knowing look and opened the door ajar.

Pillai gestured his men to carry the boxes inside. He walked back to the poor boatman and wiggled his head as a gesture to say, 'Get back on the boat.' The hapless man followed. As soon as he turned back and climbed on his boat. Pillai pulled out his revolver and shot the man on the head. The boatman fell on the floor of the boat with a loud thud.

They tagged the boat to a long distance into the sea. Once they reached deep enough water, Pillai fired 3 shots at the bottom of the boat. Water rushed in like a fountain through the bullet holes. Within a few minutes, the sea engulfed the boat like a whale eating a small fish.

Gowda took Jaswant to his lab. DRL had been served notice from the Chennai city court to shut down operations until further notice. Yet, the lab premises was not sealed.

He entered the specimen room and took out the specimen number D283/2.

"What is this?" Jaswant looked curiously at the small pet jar zip-locked in a clear plastic bag.

"Tina's tissue collected from its corpse."

Jaswant swallowed his spit. In front of him was that one mysterious, deadly thing that killed more than a dozen apes, two men, and Gowda's career all in few days.

"I want to see what went wrong," Gowda replied frantically.

Gowda took the sample jar and left the room, followed by Jaswant. "I am going into the lab. I'll be out quickly. It would be better if you wait for me in my office."

Jaswant nodded and went into Gowda's office. He had been there many times before and was familiar with the whole place.

Gowda put on an air-lock suit and a heavy mask as a precaution and entered into the isolation room. It was a bright room with everything painted in white. There were many pieces of equipment, electronic devices, chemical jars, and mainframe computers.

He got himself busy preparing the sample for analysis. He kept mixing parts of the sample in test-tubes with different types of agar. While the test-tubes were busy getting stirred in the centrifuge, his mind wandered to all the possibilities. But none of them fit. The symptoms were unique and violent, similar to no other disease known to man. Necrosis was the primary symptom, but it could be attributed to so many diseases. He started a differential diagnosis in his mind. *What are all symptoms? Necrosis? Death? Is that all?* He wondered. While necrosis might narrow the options, death could have hundreds of reasons. He started mentally listing the diseases that caused necrosis when the centrifuge gave a beep.

Hours had passed while Gowda kept experimenting with the samples and making a list of what can be the cause. Nothing seemed to fit. Exasperated, he sat in a heavy wheeled chair. His eyes were red with fatigue, begging for rest. He closed his eyes for a while, his mind still racing for answers. He didn't know when he fell asleep.

A few hours later, Jaswant woke up when the sun rays fell on his face. He had sat on Gowda's comfortable foam couch and had fallen asleep within minutes. The booze had made him sleepy. He looked at his watch. It was 6:30 in the morning. He stood up and went looking for his friend.

He stood outside the isolation room. He could see Gowda through the glass door, slumped on a chair. He knocked on the door couple of times.

Gowda woke up with a start. He looked out of the door and saw Jaswant standing there, gesturing to come out. He went into the cleaning room, removed the suit and the mask, and went out.

"What? Did you find anything?" Jaswant asked earnestly.

"Nothing," Gowda sighed in despair.

"Do you think the modified virus has done this?"

"I don't think so. Whatever we did, essentially, it's still an HIV. They can be deadly, but they are weak themselves. They are so fragile that they can't survive for even a few seconds outside a living host. I don't understand how did it break the medium barrier and transferred to others through air."

Jaswant kept silent, looking for words.

"Moreover, HIV infects only the T-cells of the immune system. How did it infect the skin, muscle, and other cells? They found, in Tina's post-mortem, that even the lung tissues were also affected."

"You know what, I have an idea," said Jaswant. "Let's take the day off. You come to my home for lunch. My wife makes this super delicious French lobster bisque."

"What's that?"

"It's kind of a soup made from chicken stock and lobster, garnished with cream."

"That sounds…umm…unhealthy," Gowda replied, making a face.

"It's delectable, but. The chicken and the lobster markedly creates a synergy in the soup, you see. The aroma of the chicken stock enhances the lobster's taste manifold and makes it tenderer. And the salty taste of the lobster actually makes the dull taste of chicken broth sharp and flavourful." Jaswant grinned like a kid.

"Wait! What did you say?"

"What?"

"The word!"

Jaswant found Gowda hysteric. "What word?"

"Synergy," answered Gowda fervently. "That's it."

Jaswant gave a clueless look.

"Listen! You go to your home. I'll be there by lunch."

"Are you sure?"

"Yes, yes. I'll be there, I promise."

Jaswant left. Gowda entered the isolation room again.

Pillai was sitting in his office. This was a day when he was not supposed to be in the ocean. He took a sip of tea from his cup and angrily slammed it on the table. "Why is this tea cold?" he roared.

"Sorry sir, I'll bring you another one," the pantry boy quickly picked up the cup and ran away.

"Assholes!" Pillai muttered under his breath. Right then, his desk phone rang loudly. Pillai picked the receiver and yelled, "Who is this?"

"Sir, there is a problem," the voice in the telephone spoke.

"What's it?"

"Police has raided our safehouse."

"What!!!" Pillai felt the ground suddenly shaking under his feet. "Why?" he uttered in a broken voice.

"I think they got a tip from the customs."

Even though he was sitting, Pillai felt the need to hold his desk for support. His head was spinning so fast, he thought he would blackout.

"Sir? Are you there?"

Pillai moaned meekly.

"They seized everything. Our guns, drugs, everything. It's all gone."

Pillai had captured a lot of items being smuggled into the country by various small and medium-sized boats. He had a fixed rate. "10 takka lagega (I'll take 10%)," he would say to petty smugglers trying to fool the authorities. If they would agree, he would let them go, or he would capture the shipment and keep it in his safehouse. The safehouse was a small hut owned by a local tea vendor Neelesh. Neelesh charged a fixed rent of 1000 rupees to allow Pillai to use it as his den.

Although, he had lakhs of worth of narcotics and other kinds of stuff in the safehouse. He was particularly concerned about only one thing. A boatload of automatic rifles that he captured two days ago from a small boatman. He was informed that a consignment will come carrying only 30 guns, and he was paid 2 lakhs to let that boat pass. But he found a lot more than that. To get a better deal, he captured the shipment and killed the boatman. But now that the consignment is seized by the police, he knew he won't be spared. The consignment was of none other than a mafia lord, Daanish Khandiyar, who was also known as DK in the criminal circles.

Pillai was sweating profusely. He stood up fast and walked out of his office.

He was stopped in his way by a subordinate, "Sir, I need your sign on this document."

"Not now. I am going home. Bring it tomorrow." Pillai started his ambassador car and drove back to his home.

He parked his car in the driveway and walked into his home. The front door was open ajar. Soon after he stepped his foot inside, he fell on his knees. His wife was lying face down on the floor. A pool of blood made a halo around her head. The small bullet hole at her left temple was not oozing blood anymore. Only because her heart was not beating to pump it.

Pillai looked straight in front. The devil himself sat on a wooden chair. He looked into DK's eyes. There was no anger, no hatred. They were two emotionless, bottomless pits, not letting out the feelings of their owner. Pillai shifted his gaze behind DK. Two fear-inspiring, rowdy men stood behind him. One of them was holding Pillai's seven-year-old son by his hair. DK pulled the boy towards him. He made him stand between his legs facing his father. Pillai was about to say, "Sorry." But no sound came out. DK held the jaw of the little boy. A loud cracking noise came out as he snapped the delicate neck of Pillai's son.

Pillai stood up and ran towards DK. In his frantic rush, he didn't notice one of DK's men walking towards him. He also didn't notice the knife that slit his throat. He fell down, his head touched DK's feet. It took less than a minute for his body to shudder one last time and his lungs to give out one last breath.

CHAPTER TWENTY-THREE

DK was sitting in his home office in his sea-facing bungalow sprawled across 8000 square feet, in Chennai. Across his large 6 feet by 3 feet wooden table, sat Devdutt. His thinning hair pulled backwards in thin streaks with his scalp peeking out from between them.

Behind DK, a bold, dark guy stood with his arms folded. His name was Rajan. He joined DK three years back as a petty minion. But with his loyalty and ability to get things done, he quickly became DK's right hand.

"How's the case moving on, DRL?" DK asked with a straight look on his face.

"ICMR has sued us in court. They have charged us for medical negligence, unethical practices in research, occupational health & safety violations among twenty-six other violations."

DK didn't say anything.

"We had maintained all the safety protocols. We ensured all our staff is getting regular vaccinations. It's purely a case of an accident. We'll win definitely, but…" Devdutt paused for a few seconds to gauge his boss's temper. Then he continued, "But DRL will be kept shut until the court gives its decision."

DK looked intently into Devdutt's eyes. He could see the nervousness and uncertainty in his eyes very clearly. "When is the court date?" he asked with calm.

"Next Tuesday," Devdutt replied.

"Who's the judge?"

"Some Peter Thomas."

DK nodded slowly and repeatedly as if making an action plan in his mind while staring at Devdutt.

Suddenly, the desk phone rang loudly.

Rajan picked up the receiver and spoke boldly, "Hello… umm…hmm. Why?…..umm…..hmmm….okay I'll make the arrangements."

He placed the receiver carefully on the phone and spoke to his boss, "Sir, it was Nikita from Moscow. Vladimir is coming tomorrow morning."

"Why?" asked DK.

"She was saying, he has been getting complaints from clients of delay in delivery. He is coming to see if everything's okay."

DK stared at Devdutt some more before he spoke, "Get the DRL up and running."

"Yes sir," said Devdutt and stood up to leave.

"What did you say exactly happened on that day?" DK asked.

Devdutt looked at Rajan then at DK and sat down again. "It was our 79th candidate for HIV vaccine research. Gowda had designed this vaccine himself using recombinant DNA technology. The results were promising and apes showed signs of delayed viral growth. But," Devdutt gulped, "but something went wrong, badly. The apes started dying. We closed the whole zoology section and put all the staff members into quarantine. But two days later, the zookeepers who used to look after our pre-clinical trial subjects, started showing symptoms. They fell sick badly. And then…" Devdutt swallowed nervously before continuing, "then they died. Their body was decayed badly. In fact, it was very shocking to see the rate at which the disease spread from the apes under test to the other ones and to humans. It takes years for a new pathogen to break the species barrier to infect a new species from the one it originated from. It was something new, something very deadly. In fact, Gowda sir was right when he stated it would have killed the whole city if had we not taken proper steps to contain it."

DK observed the research scientist's expressions carefully. Then, he smirked. He had gotten an idea. It would be the solution to all his problems. It would be the most profitable accident in history. "Do you have the research with you?"

"No. I have only fragments. I know the core principle, but the nitty-gritty of the work is with Gowda sir only."

"Hmm," DK pondered. "Okay, you may go now."

Devdutt stood up again, corrected his suit, and left.

It was ten in the morning. Gowda was sipping his tea and reading a magazine. He had an appointment with his optometrist in an hour. Suddenly, his help entered and announced a visit from DK. Gowda gave a frowning look to the clock and nodded.

Gowda looked at his unwelcomed guests and put his cup aside. "What are you doing here?" he asked nonchalantly.

"What? I can't come here to meet my old friend and my employee?" said DK facetiously.

DK and Gowda had been childhood friends. However, their paths deviated after graduation when DK got a scholarship from Moscow University. Years later, DK arrived at Gowda's doorstep. Initially, they enjoyed each other's company a lot. DK had started several businesses in Chennai and in other parts of India. When Gowda asked him about how he managed to do all those things, DK said he had found his Godfather in Russia. Gowda didn't pursue the topic further.

One day, Gowda shared his research interest in HIV vaccination with DK. He told him how he tried for funding from various government and non-government agencies but with no luck. A few days later, DK proposed to open a research lab for Gowda where he could do all his work, and DK would look after the finances. Gowda agreed readily. With this, DRL was born. Through the years, Gowda and his team presented many papers in international conferences and filed a dozen patents. He won a lot of grants that further fuelled his research. Gradually, DRL evolved into a full-fledged research laboratory that did a lot of consultancy and research works for many government and non-government companies.

All was well until a couple of years ago when Gowda met Vladimir. Vladimir was the Godfather DK talked about. They were in DK's office in DRL. DK was telling Vladimir about DRL's operations and Gowda's passion that made it all real.

Out of the blue, Vladimir asked DK, "What happened to the consignment we sent last month?"

"Yes. I am working on it," DK replied seriously. "It's stuck with the customs. There's this new officer from Madurai. He's left two years from retirement and don't want to play by our rules."

"Then remove him," Vladimir spoke with a grim tone. Then, burst into a hysterical laugh.

DK joined him too. However, the joke didn't get through Gowda. He stared at Vladimir curiously.

Two days later, newspapers showed a fifty-eight years old customs officer who was found hanging by the fan in his staff quarters. His wife said he was a wonderful husband and an adorable father. Why would such a man commit suicide was beyond everyone's might. Something about the incident didn't sound quite right in Gowda's mind.

He started digging deeper. He went through the contracts and the financials of DRL. DK had told him that Vladimir ran a research laboratory himself in Moscow. It was called Vladimir Research Lab, it provided financial assistance to DRL. Gowda found out that VRL held more than 70% stakes in DRL. And yet Vladimir was never bothered about the functioning of the lab. In fact, there was not even a single board of directors from the largest shareholder of the company.

Upon further analysis, Gowda found some half a dozen companies who placed repeated orders for drug testing. They all paid in cash every time. Some of them had their addresses in cities far north in the country, such as Delhi, Himachal Pradesh, and even Arunachal Pradesh. Gowda found it odd that firms would come to Chennai, which is at the southern edge of the country, while there were more and better facilities closer to home in Delhi and Mumbai.

Day after day, as Gowda observed DK's actions more closely, he started to realize that DK had more layers under his serious, businessman face. He tried to keep himself away from him. But he couldn't as DRL and his research were an integral part of his life. Thus, he turned a blind eye towards DK and focused on his work. However, a slight repulsion from him towards DK was always palpable.

"Cut the bullshit, DK," Gowda replied sternly. "Tell me what do you want."

DK was outraged, yet he didn't let his emotions come out. "Our lawyer wants to take a look at the research that you were doing on those little monkeys before the accident. The court will ask for it in the next hearing."

"Let them summon it. I'll submit it to the court if the need be."

"You don't understand. Our lawyer needs to cross-examine the whole research so that it's not used against us in court."

"Is your lawyer an expert in Microbiology?" Gowda smirked.

"Listen!" DK raised his voice a decibel too many, "I need that research, and I *want* that research. And it's *not* a request." DK glared at Gowda.

Gowda stared back for few seconds before speaking, "Fine! All my work is in my drawer in DRL," he spoke disinterestedly.

"I already had Devdutt look through it. He says it's not the whole thing."

"Then I don't know what is," Gowda shrugged and picked his cup of tea.

"See! Guru! I don't know what created the differences between us and what's the cause of all this hostility. But this is not about you or me. It's about DRL. It's about *your* DRL. It's our own blood and sweat that turned the whole damn thing into reality. I won't let all this go into the dirt."

Gowda knew that DK was facing massive losses as long as DRL was shut down. Yet he was unable to comprehend why he was taking a personal interest in his research. So far, their lawyer, Devdutt and Gowda were the only ones working on the court case. He couldn't understand why DK wanted to be involved suddenly. As far as DK was concerned, Gowda trusted him as much as he trusted a random stray dog.

DK was boiling from inside with rage. He had grown irritated from Gowda's defiant behaviour for some time now. He was always the last person to know what was happening in his own lab. Whenever he would ask Gowda why he was not informed about a significant issue, he always got the same response from him, "Oh, sorry! I forgot to tell you." This time also, he knew that Gowda was bluffing. There was more to the research than he disclosed to everyone. However, he was wrong. The whole methodology and the test procedures were recorded in the files that were lying around Gowda's office in DRL. The entire freak accident was, in fact, an accident – a mere chance of luck. Only Gowda knew what cards luck played to sabotage his career. Yet, he was not ready to share it with DK.

"So, you want to say the whole consignment, that fucking boatload of guns is gone?" Vladimir roared at DK. They were sitting in DK's bungalow on East Coast Road, Chennai.

"Vlad! You need to trust me. Police may have got their hands on the consignment. But I have pulled all my strings to get those out of custody."

"Bullshit! You fucking Indians don't even know how to run business." Vladimir slurred. "Come to Russia, I will show you mother fuckers how it's done in *fucking* Russia."

"Please give me some time," DK begged.

"That's enough time I have given you. You have cost me money more than you made me money since last one year," Vladimir glared at DK. "I am cutting you out."

"But.." DK said, but it was too late. Vladimir had already started walking towards the door. "Vlad! Wait!" DK galloped and held Vladimir by arms.

Vladimir glared at his arms and then at DK with his rage-filled grey eyes. His blonde eyebrows fluttering rapidly.

"What if I gave you something that would more than compensate for all the losses that you incurred due to me."

Vladimir turned around to face DK. "I'm all ears then."

"What if I gave you something equivalent to thousands of Kalashnikovs, which is more powerful than a fucking *shipload* of guns."

"And what would that be?" Vladimir asked, sounding all interested.

"A weapon of mass destruction. A weapon that is capable of destroying a whole city that is unstoppable, un-thinkable, and un-parallel. A weapon that could give world dominance to the bearer. A biological weapon which unknown to the whole humankind."

"Prove to me that you are not shitting, and I will think about it," Vladimir replied and walked away.

"He's still thinking you are hiding something from him?" Narendra Oza asked Gowda. It was their weekly drinking night when they would meet at a bar outside the campus of IIT Madras.

"He has always been the most gullible of us," Gowda grinned.

"Do you remember our teenage days and how we convinced him that we have only limited amount of sperm in our body, and we should save some for our wives?" Oza grinned from ear to ear.

Gowda laughed uncontrollably.

"I don't think he touched himself for even once throughout his teenage," Oza said mischievously.

Gowda shook his head, still laughing. "Those were the days," he sighed after he laughed his heart out.

"Yeah! Those were the days," Oza sighed too.

They both sipped on their drinks: their regular scotch with soda.

"I still wonder," Oza started inquisitively, "Why does he want your research so desperately?"

"I truly don't know. What do you think?"

"If we really believe your theory that DRL is just a disguise for DK to cover his other activities. What other activities do you think he's covering?" Oza frowned.

Gowda finished his glass and put it aside. "I don't know. But I think he's engaged with some terrible people."

"I have this wild theory," Oza said hesitantly.

"Shoot it."

"You said the virus became something totally different due to its association with Anthrax bacteria. And if you guys had not taken proper precautions, it would have gone out of control. Maybe even destroyed the whole city."

"Umm…hmmm," Gowda nodded in agreement.

"Do you think DK, or maybe his associates are into weapons, and they see this as a biological weapon?"

Gowda stared into his glass for a long time without speaking. He was analyzing the hypothesis his friend had just made from all angles. Finally, he looked up and said, "Oh my god!"

CHAPTER TWENTY-FOUR

It was about nine on a Friday night. Gowda was walking to the nearby pharmacy. Since this morning, he has had a burning sensation in his stomach. He reached the shop and asked for an antacid solution.

He was walking back to his home when suddenly he felt something suspicious. There was a shadow lurking around in the alleyway between two houses just a few metres away. The street was relatively deserted. It was summer, and it was impossible to stay out in Chennai's heat. So, Gowda got down the footpath and tried to cross the road. Suddenly, a car came out of nowhere and screeched to halt right in front of him. Before even he could react, someone came from the back and struck his head with a heavy blunt object. The pain was excruciating. He dropped unconsciousness from the shock.

When Gowda opened his eyes, he was in a different place. He was sitting on an iron chair with his hands tied behind him. There was a small candescent bulb right over his head, lighting the vast space which seemed like a warehouse of some shipping company. In front of him, there was a rugged wooden table. In one moment, he was walking on a lonely street and in another, he was in a strange place which as well could be in a different world. The change was so quick, he felt either he was dreaming or woke up from one.

He watched Rajan as he slowly entered his vision. He noticed how Rajan's gun was prominently tucked into his trouser. It was a show of power like a lion makes to force its prey to give up fighting.

He was followed by a guy with a stunted figure, light from the overhead bulb reflecting from his semi bald head. Gowda was quick to recognize him. It was his junior colleague, Devdutt.

Gowda had always been indifferent towards Devdutt. He never trusted him, even though he never had anything to complain about. What he didn't like in Devdutt was his sycophancy and his too much eagerness to please everyone. He was a gossiper. Gowda knew the moment he turned his back, Devdutt would be gossiping about him also.

"What the hell is happening here, Devdutt?" Gowda shouted on top of his lungs.

Rajan smoothly pulled out his gun and pointed at Gowda's chest.

Gowda tried hard to not show his fear on his face, mostly unsuccessfully. He was sweating. He knew Rajan was right-hand of DK, and by now, he was totally aware of DK and his potentials.

"What do you want from me?" Gowda questioned, sounding one or two notches lower than before.

"The formula," Devdutt said with his sharp, nasal voice.

"Why don't you understand? The *is* no formula."

"I want all your research and data on our latest candidate," Devdutt tried to sound dominating, while he hardly could meet Gowda's eyes.

"You know what? Just go to hell," Gowda replied curtly. "The research is gone. I have destroyed every last bit of it with my own hands."

"You're bluffing," Devdutt leaned to bring his face close to Gowda.

"Do you think I don't know why you guys want that research? DK wants to sell my work to the mafia and make it into a weapon of mass destruction. And you ass-kisser don't even have the slightest idea what would it mean for you and for everyone."

"Then, it seems there's no point of keeping you alive," Rajan said with his deep, hoarse voice and pulled back the slide of his 9mm semi-automatic pistol.

"Wait," Devdutt responded quickly. "If the research is gone, there's no point killing him. We can still find some use of him, maybe later."

Rajan shifted on his feet, his finger precariously hovering over the trigger.

"Let him go. DK might not like us killing his once childhood friend."

Rajan lowered his gun rather hesitatingly.

Devdutt went around the table and untied Gowda. Gowda gave a glowering look to Devdutt for a brief moment, before standing to leave. He walked briskly towards the door from where both his captors had entered.

"You may have destroyed the research, but we can still find the tissues of Tina and reverse engineer it to get what we want."

"The last bit of her tissue is burnt to ashes when we incinerated her corpse, and unfortunately, those poor zookeepers' too," Gowda smirked.

"Maybe you did, but are you sure there is no smallest shred of it lying somewhere around in the lab?"

Gowda turned around and started walking. "Best of luck finding it," he replied over his shoulder.

"Come on, give me a kiss na?" Nagasiva insisted. He's first time alone with his girlfriend Ponnammal in his small security room, where he worked in 12 hours shift from 6 PM to 6 AM.

Gowda looked around the whole compound before jumping from the wall. DRL was shut down for weeks by the court's order. He could hear sounds from the security room. However, the lights were off. He listened to a girl's voice and knew their guard Nagasiva had company.

The night was eerily quiet and dark. It was a new moon. A small halogen light was all that was lighting this part of the compound. Gowda positioned himself carefully in the shadows of the columns holding the periphery wall. The building was about four meters away from the wall. He looked around again and darted towards one of the main columns of the building, blending himself within the shadows. He plunged from one column to another until he made it to the main entrance into the building.

He fished out the key from his pocket and opened the door gingerly without making any noise. He let out a deep sigh once he entered the building and closed the door behind him.

He knew precisely why he was here. He paced towards the main lab where he and his team used to do their tests.

A few months back, he was in the same room where Devdutt, his assistant, was excitedly showing him the results of the recent tests conducted on the subjects who were administered the latest vaccine candidate. Gowda was not very expressive with his emotions. While he was exhilarated from inside, all he managed was to give a smile from the corner of his mouth. Everybody in the lab knew that that was not something that you could get very easily from Dr. Gowda.

Today, he was standing in the same lab, and whatever emotions he was feeling were not visible on his face.

He walked to the small wooden table in the farthest corner of the room. He found what he was looking for. He picked up the test tube tightly sealed with a cork. It contained the last bit of tissue collected from Tina, which he had used to make his post-mortem diagnosis of Tina and the other apes. He walked to the side rack where the most hazardous chemicals were kept. He picked up a plastic jar of Hydrogen Fluoride. It was tightly sealed. He looked around for a knife.

"Stop where you are," shouted Rajan.

Gowda looked up and found Rajan standing in front of him ten feet away across the table. He held a pistol aimed at Gowda. Beside him, were DK and Devdutt. DK knew there must be something around the lab that Gowda knew could give away his research. Once Gowda realized it, he would try to come and destroy it himself. That's why when they couldn't get anything out of him yesterday, they had let him go.

"I am aware of your vicious intentions, DK," Gowda said in a composed manner.

"And what would those be, Guru?" DK's voice reverberated through the empty lab.

"What you are thinking will release a curse on the human race."

"You know, Guru, you were always the smartest of our lot."

"And you were always the foolest," Gowda sniggered.

"Oh, come on!" DK rolled his eyes, "just look around yourself. All your achievements, all your accomplishments are because of me. With all your mighty mind and shiny talents, do you remember where you were until I came to support you?"

"You think I don't know why you started this lab. It was not out of compassion for me. It was to hide your own dirty work behind the veil of helping me. You used my years of hard work to launder the money that you earned from killing people and destroying lives. You have no regard for anyone. You think your life's more valuable than hundreds of others."

"You have no idea what you are talking about," DK slammed his fist down on the table and leaned towards Gowda.

"Don't I?" Gowda glared at DK.

"Listen to me, you rascal! Whatever you have against me, it's between you and me. But your research belongs to DRL. It's not only you who had worked on that thing. My team has put their own blood and sweat too along with you. So, you fuck your proud ass yourself and give that thing to me."

"This *thing* that you talk about so dearly is a failure. Your precious team and I have failed to create what we intended to. And there is no point clinging on to a dead hope."

"You don't understand," DK put all the calmness in a voice he could possibly summon through his frustration with this sick, self-prudent friend of his. "Maybe we can improve the formula. Maybe we can slightly tweak the gene-editing procedure, and this whole thing may work. After all, this was the most promising candidate."

"You leave that to me. I will work from scratch and find what we are in search of."

"You know what," DK said with exasperation. He gave Gowda a long, strange look, before speaking, "Kill him."

Before Rajan could react, Gowda ducked under the table. Rajan went around the table quickly and pulled him out. He aimed the gun at Gowda's head. "Give it to me," he said.

Gowda smirked and opened his palm. The test tube fell on the ground and shattered into a thousand pieces.

Rajan looked down. There was glass everywhere. Only glass. He hit Gowda hard with the handle of his gun. "Where is it?"

Gowda snorted.

"Tell me, where is it?" Rajan hit him again.

Gowda didn't respond. Blood poured out from his temple, crawling around his left cheek, finally dripping from his jaw.

"He swallowed it," DK said.

Rajan and Devdutt looked at him flabbergasted.

"It's a good thing then, isn't it?" Devdutt said, hopefully. "We now have a live subject to test on and isolate what we need. We have at least seventeen days to do so."

"No. You don't." Gowda said before pulling a syringe out of his forearm. He fell backwards, pulling an array of test tubes and a jar from the table. His right shoulder hit a chair, and his body toppled sideways. He fell to the ground face first. He was dead even before his head touched the ground.

"Fuck! Fuck! Fuck!" Devdutt shouted incessantly.

They heard a sound from outside. "Somebody's here," Devdutt said alarmed.

"Let me take care of it," Rajan suggested.

"No need. We have to go now. Let them think it was a suicide," DK ordered.

The trio quickly moved out of the lab, entered a room that used to be DK's office. Rajan opened the window, and all three of them jumped out of it. He used a small magnet to bolt the window from outside just how he opened it.

Gowda's suicide story was covered in a small article on the inside pages of the local newspapers. The investigation was closed even before it started. A depressed scientist facing litigation and on the verge of losing his life's work was more likely to commit suicide than anybody else.

"I find it hard to believe that Gowda destroyed his life's work so easily," Devdutt said once they were back in DK's car. It was a Fiat, Rajan was driving. Devdutt sat beside him. DK sat at the back with legs crossed and his left arm on the head of the seat. "I remember," Devdutt continued, "Gowda recorded all his observations in a tape recorder. He also had a brown diary, which he used to keep notes. Both are missing from his lab."

"Where is it, then?" DK growled.

"There is his one friend. I think his name is Jaswant. He used to visit Gowda in his lab a lot. Maybe he has something."

DK smiled as it made sense. Jaswant and Gowda had been close friends since childhood. DK, Gowda, and Jaswant were all childhood friends, but Gowda and Jaswant's friendship was at another level. If Gowda trusted somebody with his life's work, it must be Jaswant. "Let's go," DK ordered. Promptly, Rajan started the engine and drove away.

CHAPTER TWENTY-FIVE

Jaswant was standing at his front gate. "Archana!!! Come on, open the door. My hands are full."

It was a Friday evening, and Jaswant was returning from work. He was carrying his small brown leather briefcase and a packet of fruits. After ringing the bell a dozen times, he put down his bag to take out the keys. He used his own copy of the key and opened the door to his living room.

His wife, Archana, was sitting on the couch along with his son Naman. She was rubbing some brown antiseptic liquid on Naman's forearm.

Other than his family, DK was sitting on the side sofa-chair. Behind him stood a tall, dark, and muscular man with his arms folded over his chest.

"Oh! Here you are," Archana smiled at her husband.

"What happened," Jaswant quickly dropped the things he was holding on a glass table and sat beside his son.

A speeding car hit his cycle and ran away. Thank god, Mr. Khandiyar was there to help. He brought him here. He says he knows you.

"Of course. How have you been DK? It's been a long time."

"Five years. I thought you have been avoiding me," said DK in his husky voice.

"Of course not. What makes you think like that?"

"Just messing with you," he said and gave a loud laugh.

"Have you heard about Gowda?"

"Yes," Jaswant had an inkling that there was more to Gowda's death. He knew him from their childhood. Gowda was one of the most practical and reasonable men Jaswant had known. He could never commit a suicide whatever the circumstance had been. Now, seeing DK at his home with his injured son, his guts were telling him to be cautious.

"I am so sorry. I didn't even offer you water," Archana spoke, breaking the icy cold silence in the room.

"No need, sister. We will be on our way now," DK replied with a smile. He turned to Jaswant, "it's good to see you again, Jaswant."

"I hope it was no trouble to bring my son home. I am thankful to you for that," Jaswant replied.

DK and Rajan left the house quietly.

"What do you think, sir?" Rajan enquired once he was in their car, and DK took the back seat.

"He knows," DK replied and rolled the window down.

It was a Sunday morning. Jaswant was taking his family for their monthly visit to Mukherjee's. Due to Naman's exams, they had to skip their last month's visit.

But today, Mukherjee was celebrating his son Parthak's birthday.

"We need to buy a gift for Parthak," Archana suggested.

Jaswant nodded, focussing on the road. He was driving his Maruti. Archana sat on the front passenger seat, and Naman sat in the back. He was lost, looking at the cars through the open window.

"Naman! What do you think we should gift Parthak?" Archana enquired.

"Whatever, mom," Naman shrugged.

"What? Isn't he a good friend of yours?"

"He's kinda boring," Naman replied, still looking out of the window. "He always talks about studies. The other day, he explained to me each and every organ of a fish while I was eating eat."

Jaswant and Archana laughed loudly.

"Then, maybe, we should give him a book. How about an encyclopedia?" Archana gave it a try.

"He is one himself," Naman chuckled.

"Then, how about a pencil box?"

"Sounds perfect to me," Jaswant said promptly.

"Yeah, me too," said Naman.

"Okay then, let's stop at some stationery shop."

They found a small shop on the roadside. The street was deserted except only for few cars passing by occasionally. Chennai summers were ridiculously hot. Everyone preferred to stay wherever they were during the afternoons. Travelling during summers in Chennai was like walking through a world-size oven. The extreme humidity only made it worse.

Jaswant and Archana parked their car at the roadside and walked to the shop. Naman was simply not interested in leaving the comfortable shed of the car, even after multiple requests from his parents.

It took them fifteen minutes to choose a perfect colour & design of the pencil box and five minutes for the shop-owner to wrap the gift in a shiny red-yellow gift paper.

Finally, after paying the owner, they walked back to their car. To their surprise, Naman was not in the vehicle.

"Where is Naman?" Archana noticed his absence first.

Once Jaswant too mentally registered that his son was missing from the car, he cried his name, "Naman!"

"Naman," Archana, too, yelled loudly.

"Naman, Naman," Jaswant and Archana called alternately. But, Naman was nowhere to be found. They walked in opposite directions while calling their son's name.

"Naman, where are you?" Jaswant looked at all the nearby shops, but couldn't find his son.

They both returned to the car.

"Where did he go?" Archana frowned. "He said he doesn't want to leave the car."

"Let's drive a little, he might have gone to pee and then lost his way."

Jaswant entered the car from the driver's side. He found a sheet of paper folded and tucked behind the steering wheel. His heart started pounding faster as if it was trying to break the cage of his ribs and fly away.

He took out the sheet and unfolded it. There was an address on the East Coast Road written over it. Nothing else was mentioned. He knew what it meant.

Archana, too looked at the paper and then glared at her husband. "What does it mean?" she whispered, sound hardly reaching her lips.

"Let's go."

He drove to Mukherjee's house and asked Archana to stay there. He didn't give any explanation to Mukherjee and asked him to take care of his wife.

"Please take me with you," Archana pleaded. "I am dying in anticipation."

"I will be back with your son before sunset," Jaswant assured.

He started his car and drove away.

It was noon when Jaswant reached DK's bungalow on the East Coast Road. He looked at the two dark-skinned muscular men standing at the entrance, examining him with a deep gaze. They had tree-trunk biceps. Their eyes looked blood red. Jaswant wondered whether it from Chennai's heat or their anger. He also wondered how many seconds it would take them to kill him with their bare hands. He shuddered. Precariously passed the entrance of the complex and entered the bungalow. Inside, he saw DK sitting on a sofa facing the sea on the other side of the spacious room. A full-height window separated the private beach of the bungalow and its living room. DK sat with his one leg over the other, his back towards Jaswant. His one arm was lying over the head of the sofa, while the other loosely held a glass of whiskey.

On another sofa to the left of DK, sat a Russian man. His copper-coloured hair and pockmarked face with a milky white skin tone looked like a clown. He, too, had a glass in his hand, but the content didn't look like whiskey. It was transparent.

To the right of DK, sat a police officer. The three-star insignia on his shoulder strap gave away his rank as an inspector in the police force.

As Jaswant approached DK, the Russian man and the police officer turned their gaze to him. As on a cue, DK turned his head. "Come, my friend," DK said cheerfully as he kept his glass on the low-lying glass table in front of him. He stood up and walked towards Jaswant.

"Where is my son?" Jaswant asked in a sharp tone.

DK look

DK glared. "Come on, friend. Is this a way to greet your childhood friend after such a long time."

"I know what you are up to, and I know you are the reason behind Gowda's death."

"I am hurt that you think so lowly of me."

"Listen, DK! I don't know what game you are playing with me, and I have nothing to do for you. So please let me take my son home. He is just a kid."

DK turned his torso and gestured with his hands. Another big rowdy man came from the corner of the living room. In front of him, Naman stood scared, staring at his dad. "Papa!" he cried.

"You should take care of your son. Leaving your kid alone on the street. It's good that my men found him."

"What do you want from me?"

"I know you and Gowda are good friends. Sorry….," DK paused, "were. You know, before he died. He must have shared some information about his research."

"I am not a microbiologist," Jaswant replied sternly.

"No. But you were his friend. Gowda was proud of his work, he could never throw it away. Yet, all his notes and recordings are gone from his lab. If anyone he trusted more than his life, it must be you."

"We were not that close," Jaswant replied plainly.

"You were, since the early days. You two were inseparable."

"We have grown. I have a family now. He was a busy man." Jaswant looked counted the men in the room. There were the Russian guy and the police officer on the sofa. Two men were standing at the sea-side balcony. One held Naman. His pistol was prominently wedged in his jeans. Jaswant knew two men stood outside at the entrance from where he came. Any attempt to run away would be a suicide mission. He shifted his gaze again at DK.

"I don't have the whole day. Tell me where his notes are," DK said visibly irritated now.

"I said I don't know," Jaswant replied angrily.

The man at the back pulled Naman's hair hard. "Papa…" Naman cried out loud.

Jaswant ran towards his son. DK punched him hard on his face throwing him on the floor backwards. His nose was bleeding. "Tell me," DK asked again.

"I don't have it," Jaswant said.

DK gave a slight nod, almost imperceptibly. Suddenly, one of the two guys near the balcony walked towards Jaswant. He punched him hard in his stomach.

Jaswant fell on the floor, curled up in pain. The man kicked him at the side of his waist. Jaswant rolled on the floor.

"Papa….Papa….," Naman kept repeating.

DK's man took Naman away.

"Wait….where are you taking my son?" Jaswant yelled.

"If you want to see him again, tell me where the notes are?" DK said.

"Ok…ok," Jaswant said, panting. The sharp pain in his stomach was making it hard to breathe. "Gowda gave me his research before dying."

DK smiled, visibly amused.

"He told me to keep it protected. He told me that evil forces are behind it. He told me that he will take it back once the time is right, once the dust has settled."

"Where is it now?" DK asked impatiently.

"It's in my lab. I can bring it in an hour," Jaswant offered.

"Do it, now," DK yelled. "Till then, your son will be with me."

"Please don't hurt him. I'll be back."

In almost an hour, Jaswant returned to DK's bungalow. He held a red box in his hand. "Here, it is," Jaswant said before handing over the package to DK.

DK examined the red rectangular object in his hand. It had a smooth and glossy surface, with no apparent seam. "What is this?"

"Before Gowda gave me his notes, he told me to lock it somewhere that nobody can find. So, I locked it in my research."

"I don't have time for your puzzles," DK snapped.

"Wait," Jaswant said. He pulled a small red ball out of his trouser pocket. It was evidently made up of the same material as the package in DK's hand. Without warning, Jaswant threw the ball little away from where they stood. The ball erupted into massive fire five-feet high with a smell of burning plastic. One of DK's men came running with a fire extinguisher and started spraying a dense white foam on the fire.

"It won't help," Jaswant replied calmly. "The fire is from nitroglycerin, it's a self-sustained fire. It doesn't even need oxygen."

As if obeying Jaswant, the fire started erupting out of the foam and kept burning furiously. Within minutes, it went out as quickly as it started, leaving only ash and soot on DK's imported marble flooring.

DK slapped Jaswant hard. "What is this freak show?"

"This is my invention. I am working on a government project for making an unbreakable seal for the transfer of sensitive military documents. When Gowda told me to secure it, I thought it was a good way of testing my product."

"Then open this damn thing," DK yelled loudly.

"That's the problem. It requires a solvent to dissolve the coating. I thought it was ready. But recent tests on the solvent failed repeatedly. After dissolving the coating of a few millimetres, it triggered the explosion."

DK glared at Jaswant angrily, trying hard to control his anger. He was growing impatient by the minute. "How much time will it take to develop the solvent?"

"I don't know, one week or one month maybe," Jaswant shrugged. "Research is not like cooking, where you know exactly when your food will be ready."

"You have one week," DK said.

"I'll try my best. But I want my son back now."

"Oh, hell you want," DK said. "But you are not getting him back until you give me the solution."

"See, I cannot work if I am continuously thinking about my son's safety. His mother is waiting at home, and I have promised her to bring him back soon. If I go without him, she will not let me be in peace. She will force me to contact the police. I will not be able to work and give you what you want. You have to let me take him."

DK stared without saying anything.

"You know where I live," Jaswant added.

DK pondered before saying, "I know where you live. If you double-cross me, even the police can't help you."

Jaswant looked at the police officer sitting on the sofa behind DK.

"I will not."

Five days later

Jaswant looked out from his bedroom's window on the first floor of his house. He could see the grey fiat still standing at the corner of the road about fifty metres away. For the last five days since he brought Naman back from DK, this car had always been around. When he went to college, it was there. When he went to buy groceries, it was there. It had been the part of the traffic around him. Sometimes ten feet ahead, sometimes twenty feet behind. It was always there like a bad breath after eating onions.

Jaswant turned from the window to face his wife, Archana. "It's time," he said.

It was eight o'clock at night. Jaswant, Archana, and Naman entered their Maruti 800. As usual, Jaswant took the driver's seat, his wife beside him and Naman at the rear behind his father.

Their car slowly rolled out of their yard on to the road. Jaswant looked into the mirror, the grey fiat was tagging behind, like a puppy running behind its master, keeping distance.

He slowly took a left turn and suddenly pressed the accelerator to the floor. Few metres away, he took a right.

By the time the Fiat had taken the first turn, its passengers couldn't see the cherry red Maruti 800 on the street. Suddenly, they panicked. They, too, accelerated fast in search of their target.

Jaswant took a few more random turns before taking Mount Road. He crossed the Periyar bridge. He had thought he finally escaped DK's men, who were trailing him for the last five days. He rechecked the rearview mirror, and there it was – the omnipresent grey Fiat trailing them three cars behind. They crossed the landmark LIC building, before taking a left into the underground parking of the Spencer Plaza Mall. He parked his car a level below the ground in the mall's parking lot. The grey fiat crossed them and parked at the opposite side. Jaswant observed the two dark-skinned men sitting in the car for a few seconds. None of them came out. Both were tall and muscular. They wore plain black t-shirts. The one on the driver's seat also had piercings in both earlobes.

Jaswant came out of the car, so did Archana and Naman. They walked towards the mall entrance. Once they passed the security frisking, they took the elevator to the second floor. Fortunately, the two men spying them did not take the same elevator. On the second floor, they entered a large clothing store. The two men soon reached the front of the store and stood there. Archana found a white shirt for Jaswant, "I think this looks good," she said.

"Yes," Jaswant took the shirt in his hand and checked the fabric.

"Go try it," Archana said.

Jaswant nodded and took the shirt towards the trial room while Archana moved towards the ladies' section and started checking a few suits for herself. Naman was tagging her.

Jaswant entered the trial room. There stood two men already. Jaswant entered one of the cubicles. The other two followed. One of them closed the door.

"Thank god Naresh, you made it. Is this your guy?" whispered Jaswant.

"Yes," Naresh said. He was Archana's brother, who had a successful business in Australia. When Jaswant called a few days back, Naresh was in utter shock, finding them in such a mess. He couldn't say anything that day. The next day, he called Jaswant and explained his plan. Naresh had a sharp acumen. Soon after his graduation, he moved to Australia with the help of his friend. There, he made contacts and set up a thriving business of exporting and importing handicrafts. "He is the brother of my right-hand, Nana."

"Nana?"

"Nana had quite an exciting life here. Son of a Tamil landlord. His family lives in Thiruttani. People of fifty nearby villages feared Nana and his family. In a family vendetta, he found himself with a knife in the stomach of another landlord's son. Since then, the other landlord is looking for Nana. His father sent him to Australia two years back. Since then, he is working for me. This is his brother Kailas."

Jaswant looked at Kailas. His eyes were red, probably due to Chennai's heat. His white t-shirt with yellow stripes and cream vesti with a golden lining made his dark, broad face look even darker. He didn't carry the usual angavastram over his shoulder.

"As soon as I take Didi and Naman, we will fly to Istanbul. From there, we will take a bus to Durrës. From there, we will take a ferry to Bari, Italy. From there, again, a bus to Naples."

"Yes," Jaswant nodded. Although, he had run the plan hundreds of times in his head. Still, hearing it again from Naresh sounded totally different this time. His heart was pounding, and his throat was drying.

"Kailas will go with you. He will put you in a cargo ship to Melbourne. From there, you will fly to Venice and take a bus and train to reach Naples. After you reach, I will take Naman to Adelaide and then to Melbourne."

"Let's go."

"Bhaiya," Naresh stopped Jaswant by calling him, *brother.* "All the best."

Jaswant smiled and left the trial room. He nodded to his wife and walked towards the billing counter. He paid for the shirt, and they left the store with a plastic carry bag in his hand. They took the elevator to reach the parking. Jaswant drove the car out of the parking lot with his wife and son. He handed over the parking ticket to the attendant and drove away. Behind him, Naresh and Kailas were in the queue. They, too, showed their ticket and drove away. After them, DK's men left the parking lot.

As soon as Jaswant left parking, he pressed the accelerator to the floor and sped through the traffic. He took many turns before he entered a small isolated street. A few seconds later, another white Maruti 800 car came from the opposite side of the street and stopped beside them. Quickly, Archana went out of the red Maruti, almost dragging Naman with her. Kailas got out of the white car and took the front passenger seat of the red car. He put a wig with long black hair on his head and slid down on the seat. The whole exchange took only a few seconds. As soon as they had come, both the cars sped away in opposite directions.

Outside the Spencer's Plaza, DK's men scanned the traffic for the red Maruti 800. There were many. They slowly caught up to each of them to check the passengers. One by one, they scanned each of them but couldn't find Jaswant and his family. Getting angrier by the minute, they started driving fast, tracing the same path in reverse, on which they had come. A few seconds later, a cherry red Maruti 800 entered from their left. But it was at least a hundred metres away, and there were more than ten cars between them. It was driving very fast. Soon, they increased their pace and trailed the car. Gradually, they closed on to red Maruti. They could see Jaswant and his wife, but not Naman. They believed he must be lying low on the rear seat. Suddenly, the red car took a right and increased its pace. The grey Fiat followed.

Next, Jaswant's car took a rapid left turn. By this time, DK's men knew something was fishy. They pressed the accelerator to the floor and started closing on their target. Jaswant's car was only 20 metres in front of them, and they were closing in rapidly. They saw a bridge on the horizon. They kept closing in on to the red Maruti. Suddenly, without warning, Jaswant's car turned left. It struck the low boundary wall and toppled. A few seconds later, they heard a loud splash. The traffic stopped. DK's men quickly left their car and ran towards the bridge. They forcefully removed the crowd of spectators to look under the bridge. They couldn't see anything. It was too dark.

They looked at each other. Lacking any plan, they took their car and drove to their boss.

CHAPTER TWENTY-SIX

"All these years, I thought I am an orphan," Samar said.

He knew he should be happy to see his father again, yet didn't understand why he felt the intense sadness. Many thoughts raced through his mind. Was he not a good child, is that why his parents abandoned him? When his uncle told him that his parents were no more, it took him a long time to adjust to it, but eventually, he accepted his fate. Today, he realized everything he wished for in his childhood could have been true. He felt sad not for the things that didn't happen, but for those which could have.

"You have to understand, son. I didn't have any choice. First, we had planned to keep you in Melbourne only for few years. I even wanted to keep your mother with you too, but she wouldn't let go. She insisted on staying with me. For long, I kept looking over my shoulder. Changing my home from time to time, sometimes three times a year. We didn't want this for you. After many years, I contacted your uncle. You were sixteen then. He told me how good you were doing in your studies. You had even started taking an interest in his business too. He wanted you to take care of his business. He had never married because his business was his wife. He wanted you to be his heir."

Samar sat silently.

"Your mother fell sick after we parted from you."

"How is she? What happened?" Samar requested.

"Wait." Soon Jaswant was joined by his wife. Samar's last memory of his mother was of a beautiful lady with jet-black hair, caring nature, and a sweet voice. Today, the woman he saw on the computer screen looked like his grandmother. She had a slight build. Her wrinkled face was ashen and expressionless and had lost all the lustre of her youth. Samar felt pain looking at his mother's pitiful, sunken eyes. "Archana! Say hello to your son."

"Mom?"

Jaswant smiled and nodded.

"My son?" Archana said meekly.

"Yes, your son, Samar."

"Samar?" There was something wrong in her voice, Samar thought. "Did Kamla drank her milk?" she inquired.

Jaswant let out a sigh.

"Who is Kamla?" Samar enquired.

"She was our cat. She died fifteen years ago."

Samar looked confused.

"Alzheimer's, sixth stage."

Now it made sense to Samar. Tears welled up in his eyes.

"She was in the third stage when she was diagnosed ten years ago. This is another reason we didn't want to bring you. We knew that being on the run and with your mother losing her sanity, we will not be able to give you the childhood we knew you deserved. So, we let you be. I took up a lecturer job here in a local college. It paid the bills. I talked to your uncle ten years ago and informed him of our decision. He agreed that this is the best for everyone. I left with him an email address in case he wanted to reach us. He never had to, until a few months back."

"Before he died."

"Yes, he told me he had only a few weeks. I couldn't come because I could not leave your mother. But I kept an eye on you. I tracked you through your friend's social media- Mr. Wilson, cheery little young man. When I got to know that you reached Chennai, I panicked. All the trauma that I had suppressed for years rushed back to me."

"Then, you called Mr. Mukherjee."

"Yes. I let everyone believe that I died. But now I had to come forward to save you. So, I called Mukherjee and pleaded him to keep an eye on you."

"Which cost him his life."

"What!!?" Jaswant asked, flabbergasted.

"Yes. DK killed him and his wife."

"Oh my god!" Jaswant stood up and placed a hand over his head. Frustration and anger built up inside him.

Samar told him everything that happened in the last few days. It took Jaswant a few minutes to absorb the facts. Once he did, he sat down, rubbing his forehead. Archana had walked away from the computer. Samar couldn't see her anymore. "I don't understand," Samar started, "why did Prof. Gowda save the formula? He knew his research could devastate humankind, why didn't he destroy it?"

"He did."

"Then what was there in the red package?" Samar asked, confused.

"Newspapers."

Samar looked sceptical.

"When Guru realized the ill-intentions of DK, he destroyed all his notes and tapes. But DK wouldn't accept it. He thought I had the formula."

"But, you didn't."

"I did."

"Sorry, I am confused. You said Prof. Gowda destroyed his research."

"He destroyed all the tangible references, but he couldn't destroy what was there in my mind. When Guru finally solved the puzzle, I was with him. In his excitement, he told me everything. There was a coincidence which happened only by one in a million chance."

"What was it?"

"Son, knowledge is power. But it is a liability too. I knew if DK kept pressuring me, I would break. He could torture me, but I couldn't see you and your mother get hurt. It made me run away. I don't want that future for you."

"Then why did you leave the blue package with Naresh uncle. And what about the locker with Mukherjee uncle?"

"Those were breadcrumbs. I realized soon that DK may reach Sudhan too. And he will start pressuring him as he did to me. I wanted Sudhan to give the locker to DK so that he left him alone. If he reached you, I wanted Naresh to give him the blue package. They would keep running on a wild goose chase without ever getting what they wanted. But I guess, not everything goes as per the plan."

Samar stared at the screen for a long time. "I have to go now. My friends might be looking for me. Some people still care for me," Samar regretted saying it as soon as he did.

"Take care, son."

"Will I see you, in-person?"

"Not yet, DK is in jail, but he is not dead. He will not stay inside for long, and he is resourceful."

"Once the dust settles, I will reach out to you." Jaswant disconnected the call.

Samar sat for a while before he logged out of the computer and left.

One Year Later

"Where are you guys? I am freaking out," Viren said over the phone.

"Open the door, you fucker. We are outside," Zac replied.

Viren dashed to open the door. Sam, Zac, and Piyu stood outside. After DK was apprehended by intelligence services, and Piyu recovered in the hospital for a week, Sam, Zac, and Piyu returned to Melbourne. Sam filed for the adoption of Muskaan. After the death of her grandparents, she was all alone in the world. Samar couldn't bear the thought of that little doll growing up in an adoption centre. She was, in a way, family to him.

Adoption and visa processing took a long time in India. Till that time, Viren offered to keep Muskaan with his family. After a month of wait, once Samar took her legal adoption, she flew with him. Samar made a father to her. It took some time for her, she adjusted eventually to her new home and new school in Melbourne. Samar left no stone unturned to make it as easy for her as possible.

Zac and Piyu grew close to each other. After dating her for eight months, Zac proposed her on their trip to Sydney. She said, "Yes." They moved in together into a big house in the suburbs of Melbourne. Zac and Piyu visited Muskaan daily. Everyone grew so fond of her.

Samar hired Viren as the country head for his business. They set up a new office in Chennai, from where Viren dealt with local artisans for buying and exporting elegant handmade artefacts. The rich Indian art was appreciated all over the world. Soon, exports from India pulled a quarter of the revenue for Mehrotra Export & Import.

Today, Viren was getting married to a beautiful and intelligent woman whom he met in an art exhibition. She was a blogger and a part-time sculptor. They both enjoyed each other's company. After two months of courtship, they mutually decided to get married.

Three days later, Samar was strolling on the beach. Zac and Piyu had taken Muskaan to buy ice cream. Viren had left for his honeymoon to the Maldives. They had their flight to Melbourne in the evening. Sam saw the same tent where he had met the tarot card reader a year ago. Inquisitively, he entered the tent. There she was, reading the card for a young fellow sitting in front of her with a young girl. The guy had reluctantly picked up a card, due to his insistent girlfriend.

"Your karma has brought you here," the gypsy woman read, "You will be on crossroads. Your life will depend on the decision of yours and of the people around you."

It was the same thing which she had read for Samar many months back, he remembered. He smiled and walked out of the tent, shaking his head.

www.ingramcontent.com/pod-product-compliance
Lightning Source LLC
LaVergne TN
LVHW040016200726
843493LV00005B/1281